Many years ago there were .... as one kingdom—Adamas. But bitter family feuds and rivalry caused the kingdom to be ripped in two. The islands were ruled separately, as Aristo and Calista, and the infamous Stefani coronation diamond was split as a symbol of the feud, and placed in the two new crowns.

But when the king divided the islands between his son and daughter, he left them with these words:

"You will rule each island for the good of the people and bring out the best in your kingdom. But my wish is that eventually these two jewels, like the islands, will be reunited. Aristo and Calista are more successful, more beautiful and more powerful as one nation—Adamas."

Now King Aegeus Karedes of Aristo is dead, and the island's coronation diamond is missing! The Aristans will stop at nothing to get it back, but the ruthless sheikh king of Calista is hot on their heels.

Whether by seduction, blackmail or marriage, the jewel must be found. As the stories unfold, secrets and sins from the past are revealed and desire, love and passion war with royal duty. But who will discover in time that it is innocence of body and purity of heart that can unite the islands of Adamas once again?

Natalie Anderson tells her insights into
THE ROYAL HOUSE OF KAREDES....

- **Did you enjoy writing about the Royal House of Karedes?**
  Liss was my first princess and that was a big leap for my imagination but a lot of fun. And I adore a sexy boss story—the way they have to be "businesslike" in spite of this white-hot attraction!

- **What did you like most about your characters?**
  I really liked Liss's sunny nature. I think she'd make a good friend because of her rock-solid sense of loyalty. As for James, he's very saucy and I do like that.

- **Where do you get the inspiration for your characters?**
  I honestly don't know. They just appear, usually when I've just woken up. They're fully formed—but it can take a while for me to figure them out.

- **What is your typical day?**
  I have four kids so I'm a mom all day (read: slave). When the kids' lights go out, Natalie Anderson is switched on and I write for a few hours. And yes, I have a wonderfully supportive husband.

- **What would be the best—and worst—things about being in a royal dynasty?**
  I imagine it would be like living in a reality TV show all the time. But on the flip side wouldn't it be fun to be spoilt for a few days? I'd need to do some kind of work to give me a sense of purpose. I couldn't just sit around doing nothing and being royal—well, not full time anyway!

- **Are diamonds really a girl's best friend?**
  No! I need a best friend who'll talk back to me and with whom I can trade confidences and have a good giggle...although it would be great to be dripping in diamonds when we're out on the town!

Natalie Anderson

RUTHLESS BOSS, ROYAL MISTRESS

THE ROYAL HOUSE *of* KAREDES

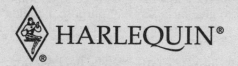

TORONTO • NEW YORK • LONDON
AMSTERDAM • PARIS • SYDNEY • HAMBURG
STOCKHOLM • ATHENS • TOKYO • MILAN • MADRID
PRAGUE • WARSAW • BUDAPEST • AUCKLAND

If you purchased this book without a cover you should be aware
that this book is stolen property. It was reported as "unsold and
destroyed" to the publisher, and neither the author nor the
publisher has received any payment for this "stripped book."

For my four lion cubs.
Thank you for letting me postpone
writing "The Adventures of…."
I promise we'll write some more soon,
but for now we're too busy
living them—and loving them.

Recycling programs
for this product may
not exist in your area.

ISBN-13: 978-0-373-12883-9

RUTHLESS BOSS, ROYAL MISTRESS

First North American Publication 2010.

Copyright © 2009 by Harlequin Books S.A.

Special thanks and acknowledgment are given to Natalie Anderson
for her contribution to *The Royal House of Karedes* series.

All rights reserved. Except for use in any review, the reproduction or
utilization of this work in whole or in part in any form by any electronic,
mechanical or other means, now known or hereafter invented, including
xerography, photocopying and recording, or in any information storage
or retrieval system, is forbidden without the written permission of the
publisher, Harlequin Enterprises Limited, 225 Duncan Mill Road,
Don Mills, Ontario M3B 3K9, Canada.

This is a work of fiction. Names, characters, places and incidents are
either the product of the author's imagination or are used fictitiously,
and any resemblance to actual persons, living or dead, business
establishments, events or locales is entirely coincidental.

This edition published by arrangement with Harlequin Books S.A.

® and TM are trademarks of the publisher. Trademarks indicated with
® are registered in the United States Patent and Trademark Office, the
Canadian Trade Marks Office and in other countries.

www.eHarlequin.com

Printed in U.S.A.

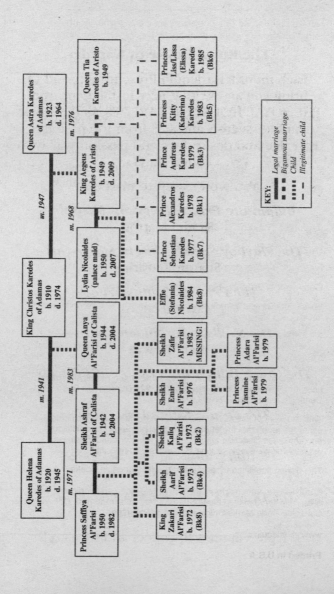

KEY:

Legal marriage

Bigamous marriage

Child

Illegitimate child

Queen Helena Karedes of Adamas
b. 1920 d. 1945

m. 1941

King Christos Karedes of Adamas
b. 1910 d. 1974

m. 1947

Queen Astra Karedes of Adamas
b. 1923 d. 1964

m. 1976

Queen Tia Karedes of Aristo
b. 1949

m. 1971

Princess Saffiya Al'Farisi
b. 1950 d. 1982

Sheikh Ashraf Al'Farisi of Calista
b. 1942 d. 2004

m. 1983

Queen Anya Al'Farisi of Calista
b. 1944 d. 2004

m. 1968

Lydia Nicolaides (palace maid)
b. 1950 d. 2007

King Aegeus Karedes of Aristo
b. 1949 d. 2009

King Zakari Al'Farisi
b. 1972 (Bk8)

Sheikh Aarif Al'Farisi
b. 1973 (Bk4)

Sheikh Kaliq Al'Farisi
b. 1973 (Bk2)

Sheikh Emir Al'Farisi
b. 1976

Sheikh Zaffir Al'Farisi
b. 1982 MISSING!

Princess Yasmine Al'Farisi
b. 1979

Princess Adara Al'Farisi
b. 1979

Effie (Stefania) Nicolaides
b. 1984 (Bk8)

Prince Sebastian Karedes
b. 1977 (Bk7)

Prince Alexandros Karedes
b. 1978 (Bk1)

Prince Andreas Karedes
b. 1979 (Bk3)

Princess Kitty (Katarina) Karedes
b. 1983 (Bk5)

Princess Liss/Lissa (Elissa) Karedes
b. 1985 (Bk6)

The Royal House of Karedes

Each month, Harlequin Presents is proud to bring you an exciting new installment from THE ROYAL HOUSE OF KAREDES. As the stories unfold, secrets and sins from the past are revealed and desire, love and passion war with royal duty!

You won't want to miss out!

Eight volumes to collect and treasure!

CHAPTER ONE

JAMES leaned back in his chair, rubbed over his face with both hands and then ruffled them through his hair. The flight from Kuala Lumpur had landed just after five that morning and he'd come straight to the office, showering and changing on site. He'd already caught up on most of the essentials and now he desperately wanted another coffee and something more substantial than a rubbery in-flight muffin. He'd read the paper and relax for ten.

Thankfully he heard sounds of movement in the office outside his door. Good. His secretary must have arrived. A little later than usual but he didn't mind; she was the best there was—usually.

He picked up the papers he'd been skimming earlier, grinning as he walked to the door.

'Bridge, did you break all your fingers and thumbs or something? The typos in this report are appalling. I can hardly read it.'

He looked up from the page he'd been chuckling over and stopped on the threshold, staring at the stranger rising from behind the desk.

She was tall, she was dark, she was stunning, she was…

'Not Bridget,' he said stupidly.

'No.' Her voice was quiet but firm, with a foreign lilt and a tinge of guilt to it.

And in that one beat he lost all power of thought—couldn't process a thing. Could only look at the most beautiful woman he'd ever seen. The only word remaining in his brain was *wow*. It seemed to take an age for his heart to beat again. When it finally did, he walked closer. The colour in her cheeks seemed to rise higher with every step he took nearer.

'I'm—'

'Princess Elissa.' He remembered now, kicking the grey cells back on. He'd told her brother he'd give her a job. He'd forgotten that in the hype of the conference. She must have been here in Sydney at least a month already?

He couldn't help himself—kept staring and stared some more. He'd seen her photo countless times in papers, magazines, on telly. But this was the first time he'd ever met her in person. He'd never thought she'd be such a stunner in real life—so often these model types were actually a disappointment live and up close, without the benefit of tons of make-up, accentuating lighting and airbrushing. But in truth no photo could capture the dancing lights in her dark eyes, or the richness of colour in her long brown hair. Hair that invited the touch of fingers, and that would feel like silk brushing across skin. And nothing could prepare anyone for the perfection of her body—both slim and curvy, womanly and tantalising.

'Bridget is on holiday. I was told to work up here while she's away.'

James nodded, still too busy processing her presence to be able to speak much.

'I'll redo that report.' The colour in her cheeks was deeper, she wouldn't look him in the eye, and as she held out her hand for the document he saw it shook a little.

It brought him back to reality. A smidge of compassion made him feel the need to give her some sort of excuse, to ease her embarrassment. 'Some of the buttons on the keyboard are probably different in Europe.'

She looked up at him then, for just a second before looking back down to take the report. Apology shone in her eyes and something akin to—panic? 'Must be.'

Fascinated, he watched the dull red splotches spread over her lightly golden skin; his fingers itched to trace over the patterns—to see if it felt as hot as it looked. Then he realised he was still holding onto the paper that she was trying to take back. He let it go and in the same instant, turned away. He'd been staring a little too long. But it had been a bit of a shock—she really was something else. Hell, he must be more tired than he thought—damn jet lag.

He shook his head, wanting to flick away the haze. But all he could see was red—the colour of temptation. It was interesting how someone who must be so used to scrutiny still had an all-over body blush like that. It never showed in the photos of her. It must be airbrushed out.

He retreated into his office and told himself to get a grip. Intriguing blushes or not, he didn't want her taking up any of his brain space. She was way too beautiful for him—the kind of woman every man would want and one who would want the attention of every man. And he wasn't one for sharing.

Liss let out the breath that had been held so long her lungs were bursting. She flung back in the chair like a rag doll. So *that* was James Black? For some reason she'd imagined her hotel tycoon boss to be fifty-ish, a little squat, balding. Not maybe thirty, tall and with a head full of slightly unruly dark brown hair. He was gorgeous. He was more than gorgeous, and when she'd looked into his eyes she'd seen the most tantalising golden gleam that had her aching to reach out to touch him—to capture it and keep it.

She should have done her research. Just as she should have taken an emergency 'brush-up-your-secretarial-skills' course on the flight over from Aristo. This was it: her last chance— or the last chance she wanted to be given. She had to prove herself here or she'd never get to go back home. She'd have to start over again someplace else and she refused to let that happen. Sydney was it. This job was it.

And what a great first impression she'd made. Completely fouling up that report and then blushing all over like some schoolgirl. She *never* blushed. But she really hadn't expected him to come out of his office with that warm smile, and the humour twinkling in his eyes. And she hadn't expected the heat to rise in her body in such an instant response. Just *looking* at him had turned her lust switch on.

Distracted, she messed up a call and mortifyingly had to ask the receptionist, Katie, to come up and explain the phone system to her once again. She'd already written down step-by-step instructions on how to operate it but still she couldn't quite get it—she was always putting a caller through to answering machine instead of transferring them to someone else, or worse still cutting them off completely. She could manage her own mobile well enough and her PDA and they were much more complex pieces of equipment. There was just something about this system. They were five minutes into it when he walked out of his office again.

'Welcome back, James.' The receptionist gave him a stunning smile.

Only a small smile flickered on his face in return. 'Thanks, Katie. I'm just going for coffee. Back in twenty.' He looked at Liss. 'Can you have that report for me by then?'

'Certainly,' Liss replied with far more conviction than she felt. But he was halfway across the room already and in another instant out the door.

Katie gave a mock swoon once they'd heard the door to the stairwell slam. 'He's back.' She sighed and gave Liss a sly look. 'Something else, isn't he? Lucky you, getting to sit outside his office all day.'

Liss nodded vaguely, not really wanting to dissect the undeniable hunk-factor of her new boss. Of course she wasn't the only one who saw it. But gossiping wasn't the way to get herself taken seriously.

However, inside she dissected his response to Katie's openly flirty greeting. The smile had been far more reserved than the one he'd had on his face when he'd thought she was his secretary Bridget. She found herself wondering what Ms Perfect Typist Bridget looked like.

'Be careful though. He's mercurial.'

Liss paused at Katie's comment, curiosity mounting.

Katie's smile was sly and Liss knew if she ever wanted to know anything about the organisation or its staff, all she had to do was ask the receptionist.

'Can't be caught.'

'Oh?' Liss wasn't interested. Really wasn't interested.

'He doesn't do commitment.' Katie kept chatting as if knowing full well Liss was all ears.

But Liss wasn't here to learn about the boss's love life. She was here to work. 'No?'

'Three dates and it's over.'

Focus on the phones, Liss. 'Can you show me how to transfer again?'

Katie didn't bother to hide her laughter as she showed Liss once more which buttons to push. 'You'll get it after a bit. You're probably not used to having to work like this.'

Liss had to admit that was true. But cut off from her trust fund she had little choice. Alex had set her up. Until she learnt to settle down she was to be without her funds, and having to work—at a job Alex had selected. For a business acquaintance of his, who just happened to be based on the other side of the world. It was so convenient for them—Elissa the embarrassment shipped off again, no longer a concern to the family. Out of sight, out of mind. They seemed to be able to do that so easily and inside she was crushed. She'd wanted to stay on Aristo after her father's death. Had wondered if there was some way in which she could be useful. Instead she'd been installed into a serviced apartment in Sydney— one of James's complexes, she'd discovered—and by the time the rent was taken out of her wages she had minimal cash left to get by. For the first time she was forced to earn her own living—to curb her impulses and to take some responsibility.

And for the first time she intended to succeed. She was determined to do a good job and to make some sort of a life for herself here. That way she could prove to them, and to herself, that she was as capable as any of them. Maybe then their rejection wouldn't matter. Maybe then they'd want her to come back. She sure wasn't going to stuff up that possibility by wasting time thinking inappropriate thoughts about her new boss.

'He'll be back in a minute and you haven't done that report.' Katie nudged her.

'Oh, hell.'

* * *

James wished he'd shut his office door. But he hardly ever did—able to call through to Bridget if he needed something. He was dreading the day she'd come to him and tell him she was pregnant and he had the suspicion it was going to be sooner rather than later—especially with this romantic cruise she was on with her husband. But he couldn't even begin to worry about that—right now he had one hell of a replacement secretary to deal with.

He picked up the pile of newspapers that had accumulated the few days he'd been overseas. He quickly flicked through, having caught most of the important news online while travelling. But he stopped at the society page. There she was—his new secretary, looking particularly glamorous in black and white, a brilliant smile in place at the opening night of some new play. He picked up the paper for the day before and flicked through to the society page in that one—yes, there she was again, smiling straight into the camera, surrounded by several handsome men. He looked through more—the same. Another paper, another photo, another escort.

She sure had been busy. She hadn't been here long and had been out every night. No wonder she could barely type a report. Her concentration would be shot if she'd been cutting up the dance floor till all hours every night. What a fool he was for feeling sorry for her. For thinking perhaps nerves had impacted on her performance. James loathed nothing more than being made a fool of.

He spread out the page of the last paper and stared narrow-eyed at the picture. Beautiful as she looked in it, he now knew it was nothing on the real thing.

There was absolutely no denying he was attracted to her. Extremely attracted. You couldn't be male and straight and not be attracted to her. But James had spent plenty of time in and around beautiful women and had learned the lesson some time ago not to take any of them seriously. Social butterflies spent their time flitting—from one partner to the next, without pause. Liss was the most beautiful butterfly of them all. She had scores of suitors—shipping heirs, media magnates—the pictures ran in every rag and glossy gossipy mag there was. And undoubtedly she'd have the knack of playing the men off down pat too. For a woman as desirable as Liss there would be no fun in plain and simple attraction; she'd be the sort to play games and to fool around to keep life interesting.

James's lips twisted. To get involved with her would be begging for trouble and he didn't need that. Been there, done that, learned the lesson. Nowadays he liked his fun plain and simple and pretty much forgettable. Nothing long term, nothing serious, nothing complicated. Nothing to attract too much attention.

Elissa was all about attention. Clearly she couldn't get enough of it.

His irritation level skyrocketed. He pushed away the newspaper and picked up another report she'd given him—it only took a quick flick to see the graphs were all hopelessly askew.

He craned his head so he could see part of her at the desk through the door. Even the way she sat was regal. Her head erect, as if there were some imaginary tiara on it as she frowned at the computer. The party-princess was playing at a real job; it seemed there was no real effort on her part. His frown grew to twice the size of hers. He'd been born into money too—not quite at the level as her family, for sure, but he could have chosen a more leisurely, decadent life had he wanted. But he hadn't—quite the opposite in fact. His family's name and money had made him even more determined to succeed on his own merits. His grandfather and his father had worked hard to build their wealth. And James was the same. He certainly wouldn't expect to have everything handed to him on a silver platter. He thrived on the satisfaction of working hard and getting the job done well. Princess out there had probably never savoured that sort of satisfaction—employing her looks, her fame and name to get what she wanted rather than doing an honest day's work. No doubt she was used to an endless stream of silver platters delivered to her by fawning servants. Well, there wasn't room on James's boat for indolent passengers—everyone was expected to pull their weight, especially spoilt princesses.

He stood, grabbed the report and gritted his teeth. 'I need you to redo these graphs as well.' He walked through, tossed the pages onto her desk and watched for her reaction. Only this time there wasn't a blush. She visibly blanched. Shying away from more work? It irritated him more.

'You need to do better than this, Elissa. Just because you're a princess doesn't mean you're going to get any sort of special treatment.'

Liss snapped her head up at the unexpected undertone of sarcasm in his voice, stared up at him. His expression was so different from earlier this morning. That glow of good humour had gone; his eyes held no gleam of gold. They were dark, cold and hard. She knew exactly what it meant—disapproval, distance.

Time and time again she'd had similar looks, similar lectures from her overprotective, over-conservative brothers. But she hadn't asked James for any kind of special treatment—in truth that was exactly what she didn't want. She just wanted to get good at her job and get on with it. Hurt because she was genuinely trying, and surprised by his sudden change, she lost the professionalism she was desperately trying to cultivate. The failures of the morning and the fear of not being able to manage burst out of her in a rebellious moment.

'Do you really think I haven't heard that line before?' she asked sharply. 'Why not be honest? You're actually going to raise the bar, aren't you? Expect even more from me than you would from others. Have impossibly high expectations that I haven't a hope of meeting.' She pulled the papers towards her and, seeing the mess she'd made up close, she totally lost it. 'The whole "just because you're a princess doesn't mean you can blah, blah" is so passé. Why don't you try something *original*?'

Her outburst was met with silence. One that stretched on and on and on.

Liss burned all over, badly wanted to claw out her tongue. She stared at the edge of her desk, not wanting to look at him, not wanting to be sacked the very morning the boss got back.

'I'm sorry,' she muttered. 'That was really inappropriate.' She couldn't lose this job. She had nowhere else to go.

Still more silence. It was going on for ever and her discomfort increased with every dragging second. She knew she'd sounded like some smart, sullen teenager, not a professional woman aiming to do a good job.

He moved nearer, coming to lean on the edge of her desk, right where she was looking. No way could she not pay attention.

When he finally spoke, it was quietly, with a level of controlled coolness that made her toes curl even more with embarrassment. 'Why shouldn't I expect quality from you? The fact is you're not like just anyone else, are you? You're a highly educated young woman with a degree from Paris, you're fluent in several languages, and you're obviously bright. So, yeah, maybe I do expect more.'

She lifted her head, surprised at his evaluation of her—pleasantly surprised.

'The princess bit is irrelevant. What's relevant is your attitude. My expectation isn't the problem. The problem is your reluctance to get down and get on with it.'

Any nice feeling was instantly snuffed. She clamped her mouth shut so she wouldn't blurt out the denial that sprang to her lips, not wanting to repeat the spoilt-child act of moments before. She had been trying. She'd been working hard all morning. It was just that her efforts didn't seem to produce any noticeable improvement.

Their eyes met and his were all cynic.

'You'd better lift your game, princess, because next time I might just try something "original".'

Low-voiced but clear, it was almost a threat. His gaze speared hers. The hairs on her arms, the back of her neck, lifted to stand on end. She watched, helpless to do otherwise, as the darkness in his eyes was slowly broken by the growth of that golden gleam. She wanted to say something—to slice through the tension threading between them. But she couldn't think, couldn't move. He too was silent, staring right through her. Despite the goose bumps she felt the heat unfurl—the tantalising yearning to get closer to the flame burning deep in him. Was he thinking the same sort of 'original' as she was? Was he seeing the shadows in her eyes move the way his were? A longing for pleasure washed through her lonely bones and in that very second the gleam in his gaze flared.

The shrill ring of the phone broke the heavy silence, shattering the moment, enabling her to tear free from the invisible bonds. As she reached across the desk he rose and walked through to his office. Breathless, brainless, she totally muffed the call.

CHAPTER TWO

THE next day Liss sat at the computer and tried to work her way through the spreadsheet software's tutorial on graphs and charts—only while it talked her through the basics, it didn't get to what she needed and she seemed to be going in circles, always ending up at the same useless info page. She didn't want to waste any more of the other secretaries' time by asking them to show her and didn't want to admit to any more people how inept she was.

Her typing hadn't had the overnight improvement she'd hoped for either. It wasn't that the keyboard was different at all. But her fingers seemed to think it was in Swahili.

It was like *Groundhog Day*—the same nightmare repeated over and over. She didn't look at James as he tossed the papers on her desk and kept walking right out of her office. She knew he was off to a meeting. And she knew she was going to be sitting through her lunch break trying to fix whatever it was she'd done wrong now.

He clearly thought she was useless. And she couldn't blame him.

She sat and slaved, tried not to get too despondent. Katie and a secretary from Accounts walked past and they saw her chained behind her desk, obviously flustered with paperwork all over the place. Liss felt uncomfortable heat rise in her cheeks at their smiles. She knew they were laughing at her expense—the princess attempting to hold down a real job and making a complete hash of it. Liss didn't like failing. And she didn't like others witnessing her failures. And here she was failing at this with everyone watching. And it was the last chance.

For some reason she just couldn't quite grasp it—she'd think she had everything covered but there would always be something, somewhere, that slipped. It seemed the harder she tried, the worse she got.

It wasn't supposed to happen that way. She thought about abandoning the whole thing altogether. Phoning Alex and begging for mercy—she'd live like a nun if he'd just let her go back home. But he wouldn't let her. He didn't *want* her there; none of them did. She had to prove herself first. So she needed to keep her eyes on the job. Not think about James in anything other than a professional way. He was the boss— capital B—and that was all.

It was the purest bad luck that he had to walk in just as she'd pushed back in her chair for a few minutes' time out. She'd kicked off her sandals and was stretching her legs out in the air—circling her feet, wriggling her toes. The afternoon seemed long, long, long in front of her and she couldn't wait to get home to her apartment, get changed and get out for a night on the town. There was a new bar in a hip part of the city and there was an invite-only opening party tonight. She wanted to dress up, wanted to dance and more than anything blow out the stale sit-at-a-desk-all-day stiffness and frustration.

Frozen, she watched as he strolled across the room, looking first at her ankles, slowly working his way up her legs, her body and finally into her face, which by now was on fire. She knew the blush must be a goodie—the warmth in her cheeks felt unbearable. Hell, she hadn't blushed like this in years, always had a good grip on her emotions—yet this felt like the fiftieth time in two days. But the flame was purely from embarrassment and irritation at being caught slacking, not the way his attention had so carefully wandered up every inch of her legs, right?

Her discomfort increased when he didn't stop at an appropriate distance from her desk, he came right up to the edge of it. Right up to her. Every cell was aware of his closeness and his scrutiny.

He didn't bother to hide his cynicism. 'Have you *ever* come across the concept of hard work?' He put his hands on her desk, leaned over it so he was talking smack into her face. A slow, satirical smile pulled one half of his sensuous mouth up. He spoke again. 'Are you like this in bed? Happy to sit back and let someone else do all the work?'

Shocked, she sat up. Stared into the gleaming depths of his brown eyes and read the challenge there.

He reached for her hand and studied her fingernails. 'You wouldn't be afraid to get a little dirty, would you, princess?'

She felt the sizzle from her hand to her heart, snatched her fingers from his. Swallowing, she tried to think of some sort of comeback. But all she could hear was the word *bed. Bed?* The atmosphere was charged and the red 'fire' button beckoned. Either of them could push it. The temptation was almost irresistible. She wondered exactly what it would take to make that flicker in his eyes explode into full-on flames. What she could say or do to galvanise him into action. She stared back and for a long moment paused on the brink of movement. Saw the almost imperceptible narrowing of his gaze as he too held back. This wasn't wise.

Despite the desire rocketing though her, she had to maintain her priorities. She was not going to jeopardise her future by being one of his three-date wonders. Not going to destroy any of the credibility she was struggling so hard to earn by flirting with her boss.

Instead she mustered every ounce of dignity she could, forcing the flush from her cheeks. 'I'll bring the papers through in a minute. I just need to print and check them.'

He stood back. The spark of something dangerous in his eyes faded and something like respect replaced it. Then he was back to reserved.

'Great.' He disappeared into the office.

Liss sat motionless for a moment. She'd successfully fended off the moment of threat—so why did she feel some silly sense of disappointment?

She counted to one hundred and then took in the timetable she'd arranged for a series of meetings he had the following week. His wary half-smile disappeared the second he saw it and any hope his expression was simply a serious look of concentration faded as it turned into one serious frown. Liss's heart started knocking uncomfortably against her ribs. She hadn't just screwed up again, had she?

'You know, princess—' the slight jibe was there '—I'll agree I'm a man of many talents, but being able to be in two places at once is beyond even me.'

It was her turn to frown. 'What do you mean?'

'Monday, three p.m.—I'm here for a conference call and in the auditorium for a presentation. How do you propose I do it?'

Liss stared hard at the paper, read upside down with a skill until now she'd never known she had. Oh, hell.

His voice cooled. 'Look, prin—'

She didn't want him to say it, didn't want him to give up on her too. Not when she was finally getting her act together and her plans in place. So she interrupted. 'I'll fix it. I'll fix it right away.' She snatched the paper back. Thank heavens she hadn't emailed it on to the other attendees yet.

He looked at her, the hard gaze seeking to penetrate her reserve while revealing nothing of his own thoughts. There was silence for a few moments. Then he nodded and she made her escape—quick.

James knew he should never have made the 'in bed' comment. Totally inappropriate. And it was because he'd been dumb enough to make it that he felt he owed her another chance. But he couldn't quite regret it. The look on her face had been priceless—for one second totally floored, and in the next? Aware—as aware of him as he'd been of her the whole damn day.

And finding her lying back in that chair, her body shown off to glorious perfection, what else would leap into his mind at that sight? Liss languorously lying in bed, those incredibly long legs bare and bronzed on white cotton sheets, her body a little damp, her face as flushed as it had been then, but this time with the glow of completion in her eyes…

The image instantly had him tormented by longing. What would that effortlessly graceful, oh, so sophisticated princess be like? How would she look, how would she sound, in the moment when her body mastered her mind and she succumbed to sensation? He ached to know and had needed the satisfaction of seeing her desire revealed for just that one second. But she hadn't followed through—hadn't bantered back. She was wary with him. Which was interesting. Why? From the papers she seemed to be full of flirtation when she was out at all her parties. Had he suddenly grown horns and a tail?

He shouldn't care. Shouldn't be interested. Shouldn't be wasting this much time thinking about a woman who would be as fickle as an autumnal day.

It was pretty obvious she wasn't that happy. He snorted. Hell, all that was probably bothering her was the fact she had to work for a change.

Now he was behind by about half an hour on his work and he needed to wrap it up. There was a function at a new bar that he was due to look in on.

Liss made a quick exit, right on closing time as usual, but he was glad she was gone. Now he could get on with his work and stop his mind—and body—from dwelling on her. It was stupid of him, when he knew what she'd be like—inconsistent, unreliable, untruthful. Exactly the kind of woman he swore he'd never bother with—never again. One fun-loving, *unfaithful* girlfriend was enough. Even now, his scars were red and sore and constantly aggravated by the day-to-day reality of his parents' dysfunctional relationship. The mess that they were simply cemented his belief that long-term monogamy wasn't possible. Short-term, sure—very short. But Liss was here as his employee, worse than that she was flavour of the month for the media circus and as far as James was concerned he'd been in one magazine too many as it was. It was totally in his best interests to ignore her.

But of course she was there, at the opening party for the bar and in full glamour-girl mode. He spotted her immediately— she was hard to miss in a stunning black dress that clung low to her torso, showing off every beautiful curve, and then flaring out. As she walked there were slits in the skirt granting tantalising glimpses of those gorgeous legs. She wore her hair out and it hung long down her back and once again he had the urge to wind his fingers into it and feel its soft length brush against his body.

He saw the moment that she saw him. She'd lifted her head in laughter at something some admirer was saying and she caught his gaze full on. Her laughter stilled but she kept up her smile. There was definitely an increase of sharpness in her eyes. He walked towards her, smiling and nodding at acquaintances on the way but, for the most part, keeping his eyes on hers. She kept chatting to the small circle of people she stood in the centre of, but, for the most part, met his gaze. As he neared she broke away, moving forward to meet him, free of the entourage. He grinned inwardly, knowing the action revealed her sense of relationship with him—sure, it was as employer, but they had a connection more than this mere socialising. He refused to analyse why this pleased him, just enjoyed the sense of satisfaction.

'You didn't tell me you were coming here tonight.' He could have given her a lift.

'You only need to know about my contracted hours, right?' she answered coolly. 'I'm surprised to see you here—I thought you'd have more *work* to do.'

He grinned. So she was still a little fired from his comments this afternoon. But he ignored the words, instead fixed all his attention on her feet and the outrageous shoes on them. Surely heels that thin and high wouldn't be able to bear the weight of a cat let alone a full-grown woman—even one as slim as Liss. They were the flimsiest things he'd ever seen—and he'd seen a few pairs of high-heeled shoes in his time.

'Aren't you tall enough?' he drawled.

A smile, one he hadn't seen on her before, curved her mouth and highlighted her eyes—beautiful, brown and deep enough to drown in. They glittered, mysterious, mesmerising and he sank fast.

She stepped forward, so the gap between them became

personal, not businesslike. Every muscle in James had leapt to attention the minute he'd seen her in the room. Now they hit screaming point. So close—he ached for closer.

She stood another half millimetre taller as she stretched onto the very tips of her toes. Her head tilted back. And the touch of naughty in her face increased, as did the promise of sensual delight.

Stunned into immobility, James realised she was about to kiss him. Her lips were parted and full and devastatingly close. He caught the glimpse of white teeth and the tip of a pink tongue. But her mouth didn't quite reach his. His blood pounded. The power of reason vanished and instinct took over. But just as he bent to meet her she whisked her head down and away.

'Guess not.' Her drawl more than matched his.

Guess not what? Oh. He got it. Not tall enough.

Damn.

She granted him a coolly indifferent smile—but her eyes were flashing with success, satisfaction and humour. He was sure she'd laugh aloud. But something stopped her—the slight shadow behind the light. The dark gleam of desire was almost invisible but he caught it before she looked away. She'd wanted to follow through on that kiss as much as he'd wanted her to. And that stopped them both from laughing.

He didn't know what he needed first—a deep breath of air or a deep gulp of his drink.

He watched her thread through the crowd of people. But she didn't disappear. A woman like that could never disappear. Anger traced through him. He refused to be the latest toy for her to play with. So much for thinking she'd been wary—in that moment she'd been an absolute minx. Ignoring the attraction between them wasn't going to work. Instead he was going to have to harness it and use it to his advantage. But he'd have to be careful. He'd only touched her hand once and that had sent a bolt right to the source of his desire. Already he knew he was going to have to kiss her. Soon.

He was a man well used to being in charge. Surely he could stay in charge of this situation?

Stupid, stupid, stupid. It took almost half an hour for Liss's heart rate to return to normal. Her overt flirt with James had resulted in the biggest cardiovascular workout of her life. If she weren't so young and in such good health, she'd wonder if some sort of attack was imminent. She definitely shouldn't get any closer. She definitely wanted to.

It was the first time she'd seen him in formal dress. The classic tuxedo did a lot for any man. For a man like James, it simply lifted him into the realm of super stud. The tall, dark and handsome cliché didn't do him justice whatsoever. It wasn't that he was the epitome of male beauty. She'd seen more 'beautiful' men. But he was more attractive than any male model she'd known and she'd met several in Paris.

James had strong, even features, above-average height, a breadth of shoulders that made Liss pathetically weak at the knees. All pluses. But the key was in his stance, the way he carried himself. Some people had an aura about them—they turned heads the minute they appeared. They had people watching, listening to their every word—charisma.

James Black had a lot of charisma.

So, one look at him in that suit and all the breath had rushed from her body. As a result her brain, starved of think-fuel, had let her do something stupid. Her lips were never going to forgive her. Every nerve-ending in them screamed for what had been so close. His mouth was full and forever curved with that charming yet slightly mocking half-smile. So tantalising. Getting in close like that she'd got a taste of his scent. Fresh, clean. There was nothing nicer than the plain smell of soap and man. Her mind decided then and there to play the movie of James and soap and steaming, streaming water and nothing else.

'Don't you agree, Liss?'

'I'm sorry?' Jerked out of her reverie by a question she almost hadn't heard, she realised she'd better save the erotic daydreaming for another time and place. Better still she should stop it altogether.

Idiot. Overcome by an impulse that had been too tempting to pass up. In the workplace she'd managed to hold back, maintain her dignity even. She'd just thrown all that away.

All she had to do was do her job well, have a nice time in the evening—nothing too outrageous. Nothing the family could get too upset about. Succeed at the basics.

So she concentrated on the party at hand, moving among her fellow guests, meeting people. She'd learnt a bit from those years in Paris—found that parties weren't just about having a good time yourself. It was much more fun if everyone was having a good time. She found her natural curiosity about people helped. But she was most curious about James. She kept her distance but glanced at him often, watching as, oozing with finesse, he schmoozed everyone he was near. But it was a genuine wow factor. He was attentive, he listened. He seemed to care about the conversations and the people he was having them with. Oh, yes, he had it all.

From his own busy networking, he watched her work the party—drink in hand. Tiny sips—the sparkle in her eyes from pure pleasure, not from any alcohol or artificial stimulant. She had everyone's name right, introduced people with titbits of info that would interest the others. She took the time to talk to everyone—including those clearly a little in awe of talking to a real live princess. Oh, yeah, she had the whole thing down pat—but with a grace so genuine it was dazzling.

You'd think she was the hostess of the place, who'd been here for ever, known them all for ages instead of only having met most of them this very evening.

His body was burning with the need to expend the pent-up energy. She'd coiled him up and then given him that one last little twist to ensure he was on the brink of exploding. He was going to have to get her for that. But he'd keep his distance for now. The paparazzi had turned up and the last thing he wanted was to be the latest escort printed in the papers. So he observed and simmered. He saw now why she liked parties— she was good at them. And that point got him to thinking. Most people liked doing what they were good at and maybe Liss would be better off trying to do a job that she'd actually be good at. Her trying to be a secretary was like a giraffe trying to roller skate—pretty much asking the impossible. But he had to give her credit—she was making an effort.

Eventually, on his way out, he couldn't resist. He was the moth, she the flame. He grimaced at the cliché. He refused to get burned, but maybe he'd get a little warm.

'Need a refill? You've hardly touched your drink.'

Liss turned towards him, away from the rest of the party. 'I finish up all the bottles later in the night,' she quipped, determined to keep things light, free from danger.

'Ah. So you start the evening as the perfect hostess and end the evening as the wild child.'

'Some habits are hard to break.'

'So I should stick beside you later on, then. I'm interested in seeing how wild that side of you is.'

Stick beside her? Temptation called again. 'Never this side of midnight. It'll probably be too late for you.'

'How late do you go?'

'As late as I like.'

His smile was sharp. 'And will you be shining with the freshness of a daisy at work tomorrow morning?'

She froze. She should have seen that one coming. 'My social life doesn't impact on my work life.'

'Is that so?'

'Indeed.' She caught that gleam in his eye and added for good measure, 'I keep the two *entirely* separate.'

His grin was wicked and he wasn't even trying to hide it. 'Is that so?' He repeated the question, dripping in disbelief, slower and even more sarcastic than the first time.

She could hardly blame him. After all, she'd been the one who'd attempted the whole near-miss-kiss thing. But she couldn't wholly regret that either. Winning that momentary burn in his eyes had been one hell of a thrill. It was nice to pretend that for just one little itty-bitty second she'd had the power over him and he was the one dancing to her tune—well, almost. He'd wanted it.

So now, having scored that point, she could let the matter go—*entirely*.

She turned, aimed for professional. 'See you tomorrow.'

He called after her with a triumphant drawl. 'You'll be on your own, princess. Tomorrow's Saturday.'

CHAPTER THREE

LISS would have slept in if it weren't for the fact that she couldn't stop thinking about James. One moment he was hot—looking at her as if he wanted her—the next coolly sarcastic and disapproving. The zing was undeniable but the circumstances were all wrong and she got the vibe he thought *she* was all wrong. Her only logical course of action was to retreat. Be cool and professional during the day and keep her distance should their social schedules intersect.

But, oh, my, he looked so good in a tux—and in a business suit. Thank heavens she didn't have to see him doing casual; she had the feeling he'd fill a pair of jeans jaw-droppingly well.

She spent a long time in the shower, the noise of the streaming water blocking the oppressive silence within the apartment. She slipped on skinny jeans and a casual tee shirt. Not bothering with much in the way of make-up. After a scrappy lunch she decided to leave for her appointment early—especially as she was determined to master the public transport system this week and not have it beat her. The numerous taxis home at night were beginning to add up and she couldn't afford to take them during the day as well. And after last week's nightmare of getting it all wrong, at least now she knew exactly which train and which bus were the ones to get. All she had to do was make it to the station on time.

She picked up her crate of goodies and headed out the door. By the time she was out of the lift and crossing the lobby she was ruefully thinking the crate was bulky and surprisingly heavy. She should have put it all in her wheelie case. Just then one of her slip-on shoes decided to slip off and skitter halfway across the floor.

'Damn,' she muttered.

'Where are you going?'

She jerked her head around. James was walking across the floor—*James?*

'To the station,' she blurted, totally nonplussed.

'Carrying that?'

She ignored the question, too busy picking up her jaw. She'd been right about the jeans—fit and firm and with that not-too-tight-not-too-loose tee shirt he was stealing all her breath. 'What are you doing here?' she half whispered, half hysterical.

'I live in the penthouse.'

'Oh.' She tried to process that while juggling the crate and attempting to slip her foot back into the misbehaving shoe. She failed at all three.

'Can I help you?'

'No, thanks.' Cool and professional. That was the way. Not ogling. Not imagining what his apartment must be like. Not feeling completely thrown.

But he'd already taken the crate from her and was frowning. 'Which part of town are you headed to?'

'Oh. Um. Just the other side of Chatswood.'

'Why are you going there?'

She shrugged, getting her grip back. 'I have some things to do there.'

His frown deepened. 'I'll give you a lift. I'm going out anyway.'

'Oh, no, thanks, James…' She broke off, finding herself talking to empty air. He was already at the lift. She righted her shoe and fell into line, going with him to the car park in the basement and to the sleek two-seater convertible he'd just unlocked.

To her relief, he didn't speak as they drove. She gave him the address and that was it—giving her time to recover, and to surreptitiously check him out some more. After five minutes she knew she was best off staring out the window. Her heart rate would never get back to normal otherwise. When they pulled up at the house, she saw him looking it over—critical all the way.

'Are you going to be long?'

Liss nearly giggled. He was acting like some control-freak bodyguard.

'A couple of hours, I think.' She'd just sit and hang with the girls, talk a little, more importantly *listen*.

'I'll be done about then too so I'll come back and pick you up.'

It wasn't an offer, it was a statement of intent and she already knew there was no point arguing. Might as well just enjoy the ride. 'Thanks. That would be great.'

Two hours later James sat at the wheel of the car outside and waited. Twenty minutes after that he got out. She'd be fine of course, he wasn't really worried. He'd got into the office and Googled the name of the place as soon as his computer had powered up. Atlanta House—a safe shelter for young mothers to stay while they waited for their babies to be born. A place where they could try to keep up their schooling and learn basic parenting skills too. A place to go when no one else would take them in.

He figured it was a charity stop for her. Of course she'd be keen to be seen doing 'her bit'—especially with her brother Alex putting the hard word on her. It was the done thing for a wealthy socialite—to be known as a great charity supporter. James walked up the path, eyeing the building with cynical disfavour. Liss's interest here could only be about appearances— only to further her *own* cause. His mother was exactly the same—on the committee for this, fund-raising for that…but the primary purpose had been to maintain the façade.

Liss was probably faking her way through every minute of her time inside there. Doing it out of a sense of duty, not any real desire.

He did wonder about the plastic crate, though.

After he knocked, the door was answered smartly by a very pregnant teen whose eyes grew even rounder than her tummy as she stared at him, and then at his car parked illegally right outside. He asked for Liss.

'She's in the common room. I'll get her for you.'

He took a step through the doorway, lingering in the hall as the young woman headed towards the sound of giggles. He looked at the notice board covered with pictures of young mums cradling newborn babies—cards and postcards and letters of thanks and progress reports. He half expected to see a picture of Liss sitting in a circle of beaming girls—their most famous visitor. He figured one would be up there soon. She'd sign some saccharine message on it and it would be framed and hung proudly. Then it would fade in the light and gather dust and she'd probably never darken their door again.

Irritated, he walked away from the brightly coloured board and further along the hall.

The high-pitched tones of the teenager carried clear back to him.

'Liss, there is a seriously hot guy here asking for you.'

He heard a muttered, 'Oh, hell, is that the time?'

More laughter, sounds of disruption, comment.

'Wow, you can move faster than lightning.'

'Is he your boyfriend?'

'No.' Liss's answer came quick and loud.

'Is he your bodyguard?' another girl asked.

James stilled as he felt a ridiculous spurt of pleasure in that idea—all the vulnerability in the place must be making his protective male instinct rise.

'Actually he's my boss.'

'Do you have to *work*, Liss?'

'Everyone has to work, Sandy.' Her tone was light.

'But you're a princess.'

'I still have to eat.'

She appeared then, in the doorway, seeming to float in on the laughter. The girl who'd answered the door followed close. Then a collection of faces filled the frame.

James stayed statue-still and stared—hardly aware of the others, only her. He was barely conscious of his smile stretching wide. Her colour was high again and the blush grew when she saw how far he was along the hallway. For a moment their eyes met. Her colour deepened yet more. Her gaze slipped as she walked towards him, concentrating on balancing the crate. He drank in her appearance like a parched man who'd been stuck in a desert for months. She looked slim next to the pregnant girl and in her skinny jeans and casual tee she didn't look that much older, and there was something different about her hair. Fresh and shining, she was even more attractive now than her glam-girl look of the night before. And for a crazy second he wondered what she'd look like with the blossoming curves of impending motherhood.

'Sorry, James, I lost track of the time. Have I kept you waiting?'

James shook his head as he took the crate off her, clearing the wayward images, as careful to avoid any contact with her hands as she was to avoid contact with his eyes. In the face of so much fertility he couldn't help the way his brain was working. The thought of S-E-X was screaming to him in capital letters. And all he could see was Liss in the centre of the action—with him.

He gave himself a mental pinch. Grow up. Act mature. Stop thinking X-rated thoughts every time you so much as glance at her. But it was impossible not to when she looked so relaxed. He wanted to magic her away with him and start to play.

'I'll be back again, soon, OK?' Liss called to them from the door after the chorus of thank-yous and goodbyes from the girls.

He noticed she didn't specify when—and the bitterness that had been blown away at the sight of her began to fester back. She'd return some time at her convenience, no doubt—probably when she didn't have something better to do. It wasn't about them, it was all about her. He worked his scratchiness up some more—it was a good way of fighting off the lust, and he felt more in control of it when he kept his cynicism to the fore.

They loaded into the car and as they pulled out he couldn't help the sarcastic cut to his question. 'Was it good fun?'

She kept looking out the window but he could have sworn her shoulders jerked—had she just flinched? 'I enjoyed it. Hopefully they did too.'

The insecurity in her voice made him feel mean. He softened. 'I'm sure they did. All I could hear was giggles when I got there.' Princess Elissa had charmed again.

The stiffness in her shoulders eased a little. 'Yeah.'

A quick glance showed a soft smile curving her lips—as if she was remembering something funny. She looked unbearably sweet and he resolved not to talk any more—not to interrupt her happy thoughts, and not to be drawn under her spell and charmed himself.

By public transport it could easily take over half an hour to get home, but in his car, with the way he drove, it was a little under fifteen. But it was still too long for James—and yet, not long enough.

He drove the car into the basement park beneath the apartment block, need eating at him—not just for the obvious, but simply for more time with her. Quiet time, quality time. He wanted to know what was going on in her head—what made her smile like that.

'Thanks so much for the ride. I'm sorry I kept you waiting.' She slid from the car.

'No problem.' He moved quicker, beating her to the boot, lifting her container out and keeping a firm hold on it. He swiped his key card to summon the lift, pressed buttons. She leaned back against the wall of the lift and her eyes closed. Her mouth had drooped. Her full lips looked pouty, way too kissable—and sad.

'You look tired. Come up and have a coffee.' The words were out before he thought further.

Her eyes flashed open and she looked at the lift controls. He hadn't pressed the button to her floor so by the time she was about to say no—and he was sure she was going to refuse—the lift had flown up past it and the doors opened onto his lobby.

'Oh. OK.'

He entered the pin, diffusing the alarm, opened the door and walked ahead of her, heading to the kitchen.

Liss trailed behind him, more certain with every step that this was a bad move but one she couldn't stop. She wasn't quite sure what mood James was in—sarcastic or maybe a more gentle one. In some ways it would be better if he was all sarcasm. It would stop her from wanting to get closer—and she badly wanted to. The way he wore jeans should be illegal, and the way he'd smiled so genuinely at those girls had been criminal. He was a thief of hearts. Alarms rang loud in her ears—she should be back in her own apartment where she would be safe. But he'd been kind enough to give her a lift; she couldn't be rude. A quick coffee couldn't hurt, could it? She'd keep her distance—admire from afar.

She stopped in the living area, with him in the kitchen, fussing over a gleaming coffee machine.

'Great view.' It looked out over the harbour, the water sparkled and the skies were blue. The quintessential, stunning Sydney view. She turned and took in his apartment—the quintessential, also stunning, bachelor pad—complete with neutral colourings erring to the darker shades, a large modern but comfy lounge suite, the requisite high-tech entertainment system and high-tech gadgets. There was also one wall of shelves—clearly the repository for anything and everything: books, CDs, DVDs and papers, magazines, a coffee cup and a three-quarters-empty bottle of red. The mishmash of colour and content was the only hint of maximalist in the whole minimalist look. She stepped closer to check out his choice of reading and viewing material, fiddling with the string of beads one of the girls had threaded onto her hair.

'Don't take it out. It looks nice.' He handed her a coffee and she lifted it to her lips quickly, not wanting to smile at the compliment. The scalding-hot liquid was nothing on the perils of James Black in conciliatory mood. She retreated to the window and the safety of the view outside.

'You go there often?' He moved to the window too—the other end of it.

'I've been there a few times.'

'So what—it's how you do your bit?'

'Yeah, my charitable effort *du jour*.' Her sarcasm matched his—but was totally made up of defensiveness. So he thought she was a cliché. Sure, she couldn't do much. But she could try.

'So why this? Why not cancer kids or the starving people in Africa or something?' Could he be any more cynical?

'They're great causes, but they already get a huge amount of support. They don't need me in the mix—I wouldn't make much difference to them.'

'I don't know—you'd bring them lots of publicity.'

'It isn't about publicity.' Quite the reverse. She didn't want it to be about her. Didn't want anyone to know. Didn't want it to become some story all about the 'princess doing good'. She just wanted to be someone—like anyone—trying to help someone else, even just a little. She glanced at him and saw the scepticism all over his face. The prickle of defensiveness rose.

'In Paris I used to spend an evening a week working on a youth line. Lots of the callers were young women in this kind of trouble.' They'd always touched her. Since then she'd heard about her old friend Cassie's hardship, and it resonated even more deeply. Cassie must have felt so alone in prison with a young baby. And what Liss hadn't been able to do for her friend all those years ago, she wanted to be able to do in some small way for others now. She stared out at the harbour and tried to explain it more, wanted him to recognise that she wasn't so self-obsessed.

'I'm no counselor. I can't offer them any advice. They've got far more major issues going on in their lives than I've ever had to deal with. But I'm someone to take an interest in them for half an hour. Someone to listen.'

'Is that what they need?'

She turned her head to look at him. He stood at the other end of the floor-to-ceiling window, facing her rather than the view. Looking so cynical she wanted to shake him.

'Of course it's not *all* they need. But no one wants to know about them. They've been pushed to the side and forgotten about. By the men who used them, by the rest of society, by their own families.'

Written off by almost everyone, a statistic, a drain on the country's resources, the futures forecast for them were bleak, but why shouldn't they have some lightness too? 'Sometimes it's nice to have someone to listen to you. To make a bit of a fuss. Make you feel special.'

While the phone line had been good in Paris because it had given her complete anonymity, here, in a city where she knew no one, she'd wanted face-to-face contact as well. So she'd enquired about Atlanta House, made contact to find out if they'd be interested in her visiting. She'd gone several times in the week before she'd started work to get to know them. To show them she was serious about being a friend to the or-ganisation and to the girls. She had no intention of flitting in and then out again. Now she'd settled into a once-a-week pattern—although she'd drop in at other times when she could.

Today she'd sat and chatted with the girls, made a few bead

bracelets with some, plaited them onto hair with a couple of others—been a complete girl. And, yes, there was something in it for her—she'd felt welcome, just as she was.

She turned away from the coldness of James's questions. 'It's not a nice feeling knowing you are not wanted.'

She gazed out the window, but no longer saw the glorious sky—too busy thinking. That was the one way in which she could truly relate to them. She hadn't been wanted by her family for years now and she'd never really understood why. So she'd acted up a bit as a kid—who didn't? And she felt hurt that they hadn't even given her a chance this time. There was no recognition that maybe she'd grown up a little—they still just didn't want to know.

Suddenly she became aware that the silence had been ticking for some time. She looked across the space, pasted a polite smile on her face. It disappeared the instant she encountered his gaze. His eyes were dark, intently focused on her, intensely burning. She'd never seen him look more serious, so assessing and, at the same time, so unreadable. The silence ticked on and as she watched the planes of his face became even more angular, his jaw hardening as if he were deliberately holding back—from speech? From movement?

All she knew was that she was suddenly, incredibly, uncomfortable. Her body temperature rose and she feared another of those awful blushes was imminent. She drained her cold coffee. 'I should get going.'

He looked down, stretched alongside the sheet of glass for her cup, and cleared his throat, visibly relaxing. 'Yeah.'

She aimed straight for the lift. 'Thanks for the ride. And the coffee. It'll help me get through the theatre tonight.'

As she passed him he asked, 'You're going out? You still look tired.'

She felt it. And the strain of spending time with him wasn't helping. 'It's supposed to be a great play.'

He beat her to the lift, pressed the buttons. 'Don't you ever just want to sit at home and hang?'

'Not really.' What would she do, talk to the walls? 'And I said I'd go tonight. I don't want to let them down.' She didn't want to be rude or for the invitations to stop coming. She didn't like sitting in the apartment alone and lonely. Better to be out and too busy to brood.

'Of course.'

She glanced at him, his face had closed over again. That touch of sarcasm was back and as the doors closed, separating them, she heard it even more in the slow drawl. 'Have a good night.'

He called her into his office the minute she appeared—ahead of time—on Monday morning.

'Princess, let's be honest.'

Oh, no, he was looking serious. She realised the whole work life/social life being separate stuff was accurate in James's case. He'd smile charmingly at drinks and then sack her without a qualm the next working day.

'The secretary thing.'

Oh, no. He *was* going to sack her.

'It's not working out.'

'I'd thought…' She stumbled over her words, felt the flood of fire in her face. 'I'd *hoped* I was improving.' Dignity, where art thou? She didn't want to be sent back to where she wasn't wanted. Wasn't she ever going to be wanted anywhere? And she really had been trying. Really.

'There's something else I think you could do for me.'

She paused, for a second her thoughts going totally inappropriate and her internal heat sizzling.

'I have a new hotel opening on Aristo in a few weeks.'

Aristo?

'We're having a party there to herald the opening at the end of next week.' The corners of his mouth lifted. 'Do you do parties, princess?'

'You know I do.' He wanted her to go to a party? What, once she was home and fully in disgrace? She wouldn't be home for long—Alex would probably pack her off again to another far-flung destination before she even had the chance to get over the jet lag.

'I want you to take over the planning. I want exclusive. I want glittering.'

She dragged her attention back from the pool of self-pity. He wanted her to *organise* it? The mother of all parties?

'I want a gala ball unlike any other. I need VIPs in attendance and international media to cover it. I want the place dripping in glamour and a spread in every magazine and newspaper on the planet.'

Her heart started thundering and for once it wasn't because of the way he was looking at her—not entirely anyway. 'OK. You'll have it.' She beamed at him, her mind already whirring with wicked ideas. There was nothing she loved more than a big party—and this one was hers to create.

'Go.' He jerked his head towards the door, his matching smile seemingly reluctant—a little indulgent. 'The file is in the system—you'll find the budget details there and the preparations that have already been made. Look them over and make any adjustments you see fit. This is your party, princess. You make it work.'

'Yes, boss!' She answered smartly, but practically skipped out of the room.

'Princess.'

She stopped and turned. His smile was gone and there was a serious message in his eyes.

'Don't make me regret it.'

CHAPTER FOUR

JAMES wouldn't regret it. He'd spend the rest of his days congratulating himself. In her mind Liss saw it all—a fabulous success that would be talked about for years to come. A sumptuous, elegant event that no other could match and where the invitations were prized higher than the rare pink diamonds of Calista.

And it was on *Aristo*. Bittersweet anticipation burned through her. Finally she'd be able to see Cassie. She'd gone home for her father's funeral but Alex had had her packed and out of there again before she could blink, let alone trace her old friend. And now that Seb had found her and their son, there was so much to celebrate. Liss still couldn't believe she had a nephew—or that her friend had been through so much. She ached that she hadn't been able to see them sooner.

The speed of her ejection from Aristo still stunned her but hopefully, if she pulled something magical off with this party, she might show them all what she was capable of, maybe then she'd be more welcome there.

She pushed the chaos of emotion aside. Decided to start with the fun stuff. The invitations themselves had to be something special. They'd give some clue to the style of the event and set up the expectations of the guests. She needed the most glam guests too. It took no time at all to compile a list of Aristan dignitaries and socialites who she knew would seal the exclusive nature of the event. The elite circle that in itself drew crowds.

She flicked over the file James had mentioned and decided to change most of the things already in place. Just under two weeks wasn't long to arrange things the way she wanted, but she knew she could pull it off. She surfed on the Internet for ideas, and chose to ignore the fact that the new temp brought in to cover the secretarial duties she'd now abandoned had mastered the phone system and the internal accounts system in less than an hour.

If James wanted the best, she would give him the best. The finest foods, the finest wines, the finest décor—utter opulence. In a city of excess and extreme wealth it needed to be some party to impress the jaded palates of the Aristan elite.

James was surprisingly hands-off in his management of her. All morning he left her to her own devices. She was pleased; she wanted to keep much of what she was planning under wraps so when all was revealed on the night it would have maximum impact. Because the person she wanted to impress most of all was him. She wanted him to lose that touch of sarcasm once and for all. Wanted him to be the warm, welcoming boss he'd been that first day when he'd thought she was his usual secretary.

Who was she trying to kid? What she really *wanted* was him—full stop. And that, she knew, wasn't wise.

She watched as he walked out for lunch. The minute he'd gone she escaped the office too. There were some boutiques nearby she often browsed through—including a fabulous shoe store that had several styles she was eyeing up. Today was a good day—worthy of celebration, and that pair in particular called to her from its perch in the left-hand corner of the window. Temptation was too strong. She had to try them on. And then, of course, once she'd tried them on, she had to own them. Handing over her credit card, crossing fingers that she hadn't already maxed out the limit, she bought the soft slip-ons with her current favourite style of slim but very high heel. And, like all eager and true shoe lovers, there was no way she was leaving the store without them on her feet.

She laughed at her folly. But there was a lot to be said for retail therapy—it could be a temporary filler for her hunger for something else entirely.

As a result of the impulsive spree, she was a little later than she intended on her return to the office and found the door downstairs being held for her by James.

He glanced at the bag in her hand and then at her feet. A gleam, it could only be of amusement, put the golden touch to his chestnut eyes. 'What is it with you and shoes? They're ridiculous.'

'No, they're not.' They were gorgeous, and felt light and cool on her feet. And sexy.

'Suitable for five minutes' standing and nothing more.'

'I can do anything in these shoes,' she declared rashly.

An eyebrow quirked and the gleam became decidedly devilish. 'Anything? Race me up the stairs, then.'

Her chin lifted and adrenalin kicked through her body. 'I'm actually pretty fast.'

His smile widened more but the reply was slow and mock-ing. 'That I can believe.'

Her eyes narrowed; the need to justify herself galloped through her. She turned and faced the flight of stairs. 'Marks, get set, GO.' She took off and was aware of nothing moving at her side. At the top of the first flight she stopped and looked down to where he stood watching. 'Why aren't you racing?'

'I'm giving you a head start. Those shoes really are a handicap.'

'More fool you.'

She ran, light-footed and quick. But he, unlike she, could leap up three or four at a time. While her legs were long, she had to tackle the stairs one at a time, for fear of, well, breaking an ankle.

Naturally it was no time at all before he'd bounded by her side and in front. He stopped on the next landing.

'Overtaken on the third flight,' he mocked. 'Admit it, barefoot you'd be better.'

'My shoes are part of my self-expression.'

'Beautiful and decorative and entirely unsuitable for anything useful.'

She could feel the flush. Frustration merely made it worse. 'Actually I prefer to think of them as a little different, a little dangerous and definitely desirable.'

His smile sharpened. 'Definitely,' he repeated softly. 'But I still think you'd be better off without them.'

He kept walking and she tried to hold her ground, but as he came right into her space she couldn't stop her steps back. He followed, and she kept backing until there was nowhere to go unless she was suddenly imbued with the power to walk through walls.

'What are you doing?' Did she have to sound so breathless still?

'I'm the winner. I'm collecting my prize.'

OK, so *now* she was breathless. 'We didn't get round to discussing prizes.'

'No. So we didn't.' He looked thoughtful. 'I won. I get to

choose.' He grinned—looked as if he'd decided. 'What does the hero always ask of the princess?'

'I'm not sure you could be called a hero.'

'A kiss,' he declared and didn't bother to address her point. 'It's always a kiss.'

'I don't think that's a good idea, James.' It was a moment of cool sanity in the heat of her vexation and failure. She refused to let the knot of desire inside uncoil.

His eyes narrowed. 'There's no crowd for you to hide behind now. You're actually going to have to deliver.'

So he was still thinking of the near-miss kiss too. She'd thought of not much else every night since in her apartment with its soulless walls and its big lonely bed. She'd got so close, pulling away like that had left more regret than she'd expected.

He rested his hands on the wall either side of her head. His body a hard plane leaning slightly over hers. The ambient temperature spiked. Despite her reluctance a wave of want washed over her.

'This isn't a good idea,' she repeated. But she couldn't quite bring herself to say no.

She couldn't be sure he'd hear her anyway, he was staring so intently at her mouth, seeming so focused as to be oblivious to everything else.

'I know,' he muttered.

Regardless of that admission, he lowered his head. She kept her eyes open so she could see him right up close—the faint darkness on his jaw where his stubble was starting to show, the fringe of thick lashes over those golden lit brown eyes, the fullness of lips.

He too kept his eyes open—barely. Golden lights gleamed beneath his lashes and all she wanted was for them to move closer. He didn't press his mouth to hers immediately. For a moment that felt like for ever he stood, lips a millimetre from hers, until she was the one who made the first minuscule move—almost unconsciously, a tiny lift to her chin.

At that his tongue flickered out and touched the corner of her mouth. Then his lips descended that last infinitesimal distance. Soft and gentle at first, then any sense of reluctance vanished. In that instant the pressure was harder and the sensations deeper and suddenly it was no sweet, simple kiss but one that was hard and hot and hungry and without end.

Some time ago her eyes had shut, she didn't know exactly when, but now it was dark and velvety and warm and with every timeless moment she felt herself slipping further under the spell of sensuous desire that he was weaving.

He was good. Oh, yes, he was very, very good.

She thought he was about to pull away so she moved. Pushed fingers through his thick hair, holding him near so she could keep kissing him, keep him kissing her.

Their noses brushed and hers was filled with his clean soapy smell. Her body arched, seeking the strength of his. His hands were still planted on the wall behind her. She wanted him to move, wanted them on her. She could sense the strength in the arms that made bars—a prison she had no desire to escape from. She just wanted the bonds to be tighter and right around her.

She arched her body closer to his again, restless and irritated that he was out of reach. His lips left hers, but only so they could press kisses along her jaw and she groaned, not wanting the deep kiss to stop, but at the same time wanting him to explore all of her the way he was now exploring her neck. At the sound he returned to her mouth, his tongue at first toying and then taking. She opened for him and fought back, her fingers twirling through his hair, her tongue twisting round his.

She was unprepared for the sudden slam of his body as he flung forward, melding his body length against hers. The impact was a shock, but one of pure pleasure, forcing from her a cry of surprised delight, followed by a sigh that blatantly asked for more.

She tried to breathe but he was there and taking deeper from her, not giving her the chance to get oxygen—no chance to clear her head. She spread her legs a fraction more and he pushed closer so his hard thigh hit the spot she needed it to.

Chest to chest, hip to hip, the hunger in her belly roared. She moaned again, twisted against him, wanting closer, wanting naked, wanting complete consummation.

He pressed against her and his body was as hard and strong as she'd imagined. Hers grew softer, shifting, making space for him, her curves melting into his planes. Yet inside the tension of desire was pulling ever tighter and her muscles wanted to move. The kisses grew even more fiery. Passion, more raw, more extreme than she'd known.

She couldn't stop the instinctive rocking of her hips, only able to make tiny movements she was so squashed between the concrete wall behind her and the even harder pressure of his body up against hers. The pleasure and the torture were too exquisite. She thought he was as turned on as she, his body was so rigid and she was sure she could feel him shaking while he took possession of her mouth with his tongue. Oh, his tongue and his lips tasted of paradise and they alternately nibbled and devoured her. She moaned again under the onslaught of sensual pleasure, the promise of carnal delight and she couldn't wait much more. She wanted that tongue everywhere; she wanted *him* everywhere. She wanted it all, right now.

And then he was gone. Wrenching his head free of her

hands, which were roughly tugging through his thick hair, he stepped back, whirled round and planted his back on the wall next to hers. He rammed both fists beside him onto the cool concrete. It must have hurt. Side by side they stood. Silent save for the rush of breathing and the fight to get it back to normal speed.

Finally James spoke. Quick, rough, all banter banished. 'You were right.'

Bemused, she turned her head, wanting to read his expression. But side on she saw nothing but the set of his jaw and lowered lids as he scrutinised the stairs going down ahead of them.

She just wanted him to step closer again.

His frown deepened and when he spoke again the words impacted much more clearly. 'That wasn't a good idea.'

A chill feathered over her—making goose bumps rise on her overheated skin. For all her supposed wild-child ways she'd never contemplated sex in a stairwell before. And one minute ago she hadn't just been contemplating it, she'd nearly begun to beg. She'd been the one moaning; she'd been the one rocking against him; she'd been the one to incite it all. He'd just stayed tight and hard—right up against her. Except for his tongue, which he damn well knew how to use, he hadn't been moving at all.

And he was regretting even that already. Here she was feeling both shattered and completely turned on and he was thinking, uh oh, bad move. It was written all over him—in the way he'd thrust *away* from her, not into her as she'd wanted.

Humiliation seeped through every cell. Had she turned him *off*? He'd only asked for a kiss and she'd offered him everything on a platter. Side order of fries and free dessert included—all at once. Too far, too fast.

And he wasn't interested. Right now he wouldn't even look at her.

'Then let's just forget it ever happened.' That sure was what she intended to do. With cold precision she moved forward, up the last flight of stairs to where their offices were.

He didn't reply, didn't follow. Didn't appear in the office for another twenty minutes—during which time she'd managed a side trip to the bathroom to fix her face and hair. She winced at her reflection—all big eyes and puffy lips and hard nipples.

When he walked back into the office suite he didn't acknowledge her. Just nodded generally in the direction of her and the temp secretary, stalking straight into his office and closing the door. Clearly he'd paid a trip to the little room too because his hair wasn't sticking up the way it had after she'd had her fingers through it.

She'd never had an experience where she'd slipped so out of control. As far as he'd be concerned she'd have proved herself right on one thing only—that she was pretty fast. But he'd never know that that was only with him. She wasn't going to make a fool of herself like that again.

Utterly mortified she sat and forced herself to focus and work hard on the arrangements. She refused to fail now. It was precisely what they all expected her to do. Even James. *Especially* James.

Now more than ever, she needed to prove him wrong.

CHAPTER FIVE

THE exhibition opening at the contemporary art gallery was a do that many of the socialites had been hyped up about for days. It was going to be the *most fabulous* party, darling, everyone who was anyone was going to be there—the Premier of the State, the actors, the models and, yes, even the newest princess in the city.

Liss had been looking forward to it simply for the fun it promised, but now she was even keener given her current task. If it was that fabulous then she wanted to know why. What was it that made one party so much more successful than another? She intended to start analysing, not just enjoying.

She arrived only a little late and looked around, taking in the décor, the drama of the entrance, the ambience and atmosphere as well as the practicalities—who took the coats and bags and where they put them, how the drinks were being served and the nibbles were being presented. She slowly walked around the perimeter, for once not going straight into the centre of the action. Instead she stood back, trying to take in the whole picture.

'Taking notes?' An all-too-familiar sarcastic voice at her shoulder finally made her pay attention to the other guests—well, one in particular.

She turned slowly to face him, giving herself time to hide the involuntary smile. The sight of him in a tux would always make her smile and her body sizzle—she mentally dove into a tub of ice. 'As a matter of fact, yes.' She registered the wariness in his expression and chilled down further.

'Tell me what you see, then. What can you learn from this party?'

She decided to take the question at face value and ignore the suggestion of cynical disbelief. 'I like the way there are so many wait staff no one is going to have a problem getting a drink or something to snack on.'

He didn't look overly impressed. 'I guess it's always good to satisfy appetites. You wouldn't want anyone to be left hungry for more.'

She shot him a quick sideways look but his face was bland.

'Actually hungry for more is a good thing,' she declared, determined not to agree with him. 'Having enough, or, worse, overindulging, can leave a sickly taste. You want them to look back on the night wishing they could have had more, could have stayed for longer. Wishing there was another party just like it the next night.'

'But there won't be, will there? The situation can't be replicated. So aren't you in danger of everyone leaving with a feeling of disappointment?'

'All good things must come to an end.' She fell back on cliché. 'Better to have everyone finish on a high rather than overtired and no longer wanting the indulgence.'

He stared at her for a moment too long and her discomfort increased. They were just talking parties, right? Because if they weren't, she felt the need to point out he was the one who'd broken up their own little private party the other day a tad early for her liking. She was the one left disappointed. She was the one reliving humiliation now with warming cheeks.

Rapidly she moved on to another point. 'But the music is too loud, that's a basic no-no. People can't hear each other talk.'

'Do they really want to talk, though? And if they do, they have to get closer to hear. Isn't that a good thing?'

She looked at him, realised he was standing closer than convention and felt the heat rise more. 'It rather depends on what you want to get out of the occasion. What's the point of the party?'

'All the best parties are the ones where people hook up.' His smile made an appearance—the caustic one. 'And it gives the other guests something to talk about. They all love a little gossip.'

He looked around, seeming to enter the spirit of analysis while she tried to figure him out. Was he flirting? Quite what they were analysing and why was a little fuzzy to her. That, combined with the aftermath of the kiss earlier in the week, had her on the defensive.

'What about the lighting? It's a little bright, isn't it?' he asked.

'It's an art gallery, James.' She relished the rare opportunity to make a comment as witheringly as he so often did.

'Yeah, but it could be more subtle. More intimate. Intimate at parties is good.'

'Why?'

'So people can relax, get to know each other. Have a good time.'

She decided his provocative talk was deliberate, knew she should ignore him, but she couldn't help biting. 'Tell me, James, is it a party I'm planning for you or an orgy?'

By now the wary look had completely vanished and his eyes were brimming with appreciation. She refused to look at his mouth with its broad smile and white teeth and the glimpse of tongue—now she knew what that tongue could do.

'An orgy? There's a thought. Lots of nymphs on order?'

That really got her back up. She wasn't interested in being at a party where his main aim was to eye up the talent. 'I'm not sure I can do this job for you, James. It seems it's a dating service you want.'

'Actually, no, I don't need help getting dates. But I am surprised to find you standing alone like this. Where's your posse of admirers?'

'Posse?'

'Yeah.' Suddenly all humour was gone. His eyes had gone like daggers. 'Ever thought you might be better off with quality rather than quantity?'

Liss clammed. Exactly what was he implying? She'd learnt to be careful when it came to men. There were guys out there more than happy to kiss and tell—packs of lies. While she didn't much care what the rest of the world thought, she did find it easier to go out with an assortment of men—allowing none of them too close. It kept them, and everyone else, guessing and none of them were able to assume privileges or presume intimacy.

But it did upset her that those who were supposed to be closest to her—who ought to know her better than anyone—chose to think the worst. This was why her brothers' heavy-handedness rankled. She might be a party girl, but she wasn't promiscuous. Was that what James thought?

That kiss had been a colossal mistake. She'd never reacted like that before—never wanted someone with that rough and ready and right-now-before-the-excitement-kills-me kind of wanting. Did he think that she'd be like that with just anyone? Staggered at the idea, she painfully recognised what it meant—he really did only see her as a shallow party princess.

The silence had gone on and she was too thrown to think of a comeback. But then it seemed he lowered his sword. He looked back around the room again. 'OK. What else can you tell me? How else could this do be better organised?'

She focused on the question. 'There isn't enough seating—the age range here is wide and frankly most women like to sit down and have a good old gossip now and then. Getting the balance right between too much seating and making the guests move and mingle can be tricky. I don't think they've got it right here. And not only is the music a little too loud, it's not a great selection—I know we're in an avant-garde gallery and they're setting the scene, but even a little melody would be good. This stuff is just noise and it's not helping people relax. On the other hand, *I* think the lighting is excellent—it draws your eye to the pieces on show, which is the point of the party after all. Lastly I think the cocktails are delicious.'

She actually saw a smile on his face—a genuinely warm one. But in the next instant the softness left his eyes and caution re-entered.

'About the other day…' His voice lowered, became serious.

He wasn't going to do a post-mortem, was he? She'd dissected and analysed every moment of that kiss enough already. That and his subsequent speedier-than-lightning escape. She wasn't about to have him shovel another pile of dirt on an episode she'd already tried to bury. So she cut him off.

'Like I said, let's forget about it.' She spied someone she could beaver over to and engage in meaningless conversation. 'I already have.'

For a moment something flashed in his eyes, then he

battened whatever it was down, so the light dimmed and it was all cool darkness staring at her.

'Is that so?'

'Of course.' She dug deep for a synthetic smile. 'It was just a kiss, James. Nothing to get too excited about.' With that flippant remark she left him, off to find a few of those cocktails and drown the taste of the great big lie she'd just told.

James stared after her for a few seconds and then turned away in disgust as she nabbed a glass from a clearly wowed waiter and walked, all smiles, up to some jerk with purple spiked hair. If that had been 'just' a kiss then he was more of a fool than he'd realised. How could she be so blasé? As if that sort of meltdown happened any old day? Not to James it didn't. Kisses sure, but not a full-throttle combustion that had nearly had him on his knees and begging for more.

Hell, she really was just like his ex, Jenny. Shallower than an inflatable paddling pool and more fake than half the boobs in Brazil. But she hadn't felt like a fake. Her kiss had been hot and surprisingly sweet and he'd immediately wanted more—more kisses, more contact. The feel of her lithe body, tight but softening against his, the way her fingers had held him close, the little moans of lust—all had combined to make him lose it completely.

It hadn't been 'just' anything. She'd gone up in flames and he'd nearly been burnt alive. He'd been shaking with the effort to stop ripping clothes aside and plunging deep into her body the same way he was thrusting his tongue into her hungry, melting mouth. She'd been willing and compliant and offering everything. He'd wanted to take her up on it in a way that was instant and painful. It had only been the cool concrete he'd been pressing his curled fists on that had stopped him—

the hard reminder of where they were. Once he'd been free of her wild embrace, reason had returned.

And thank God he had stopped. When she now claimed it to have been so meaningless, so everyday, so *forgettable*. The thought of her bestowing kisses like that on just anybody made his blood boil. *Stupid.* He knew this already—she was the type to be ready and willing to turn it on with whoever she fancied in the moment and with no concept of loyalty or depth.

How good a time did she have with all those guys she was photographed out with? He didn't want to think about it. That way, torture lay—he'd been through that before and he'd be a damn fool to set himself up for it again.

Seeing her at the centre of yet another adoring crowd, he decided he wasn't going to stick around to watch any longer. She was still in full flight—not looking at all worse for wear, not a hint of tiredness about the eyes. Right now he felt tired just looking at her. Vivacious, sparkling, drawing everyone to her—men, women, gay, married, straight. They all flocked to her. And it wasn't just the 'princess' factor. She was a fabulous guest. She didn't dominate the conversation but she sure kept it sparking. Somehow she made everyone around her feel good.

Everyone except James.

He could see how she thrived on it—the brightness in her eyes was evidence of her enjoyment. Why was it she needed this so much? To be celebrated. To be adored. It seemed such a false sort of existence. Did she really think these people were all offering true friendship? What if she weren't beautiful, if she weren't a princess? Did she really think they'd still be there for her?

And her assessment of the event tonight had been pretty astute. He'd played devil's advocate partly for the fun of it, partly to test her. And she'd done well. It added to his impression that she was more capable than she gave herself credit for. That added to his vexation.

It really was time for him to leave. Not intending to talk to Liss or anyone else at the party again. His convivial spirit had gone into hiding. But just as he hit the exit she came up to him and this time her smile was the one dripping with sarcasm.

'Has the clock chimed? Is it pumpkin time already?'

'I have to work in the morning. I take that seriously.'

'Tomorrow's Saturday, James.' She smiled in triumph.

'I know, princess, but it's still Friday in Europe, so in the morning I work.'

She actually looked concerned. 'It is possible to work hard *and* play hard, you know.'

'Maybe. But you know you can do more than this, Liss. You *should* do more than this.' He didn't know why she bothered him so much. Why should he even care? But he did and it pissed him off even more. 'You're wasting the talents you have. You're wasting your life.'

Liss just held back the gasp. Froze over, trying not to let her face or body reflect the strike of hurt. Wasting her life? In other words she was a waste of space.

His eyes narrowed. 'All you're interested in is whatever feels like fun right now, and don't you give a damn about consequences or tomorrow.'

'There's nothing wrong with enjoying a party, James.' He could never understand what her life was like. How alone and lonely she increasingly felt. Homesick for a home she no longer had. All the most fabulous parties in the world could never make her feel better about that. But they helped. And the people welcomed her with open arms—unlike her family.

'But that's all you do, isn't it? You're spoilt, Elissa. A lost little girl.'

At that point her temper became stronger than her grip on it. 'Must you be so patronising? Who are you to pass judgment on me anyway? What business is it of yours?'

'None. Except when the way you party impacts on my business.'

'I'm at work on time every day.'

'And doing a sterling job.' Devastatingly sarcastic.

'You don't think I can do it, do you?'

'Well, I have yet to see much evidence to the contrary. You say you can work hard, but you're still showing up barely on time, leaving the minute the clock strikes, spending every spare moment shopping.'

'What I do outside of work hours—'

'Spare me. I already know. But you're not putting the effort in work hours either. You're playing at it. In between reading magazines and surfing the Internet, you still haven't even figured out the phone system.'

He *knew* that?

She stared at him—at the anger in his gaze. What had she done to make him dislike her so much? And yet even as she watched she saw it transmute into something else. The magnetism that was so strong between them grew: desire. Need threaded with frustration and ran through her veins, excitement and longing rushed. As the room seemed to darken— there was only James.

The flash of light broke the spell. Just as she registered the clicking sound, James swore, short and crude, his lips barely moving. He stepped away immediately. Turned a final, fleeting, burningly cold glare at her as he exited. Liss blinked— forcing her focus away, suppressing the desire to follow him; instead she faced back to the party, lips twisting up automatically for the camera.

CHAPTER SIX

JAMES barely slept. The grumpy, headachy mood didn't improve when he thought about the night before. He should be working—making those calls. He should be concentrating. Instead he was hit with hideous memories. He remembered clearly his mother's beseeching tones.

'You know I love your father very much,' she'd said.

He'd started walking.

She'd called after him. 'You know I love you…'

He'd started running then. Yeah, sure you do, *Mother*. Whose dictionary were you looking up love in? Family and loyalty clearly meant so much. Not.

He got out of bed and went to the gym. Still couldn't stop thinking, sweating out old hurts, swamped with the threat of new ones. In his mind the past got all mixed up, the hurt, the anger of loss and betrayal. The humiliation of deception and discovery and being the last in the world to know.

His mother had done it. Jenny had done it. Liss was of the same ilk—needy for attention. One man would never be enough. He told himself and told himself—warning. And yet he couldn't keep away. The drive to be physically near her was too strong. And even though he had spoken the truth last night, he felt guilty.

She opened the door, clearly surprised to see him. She looked him up and down a couple of times. Made him feel so self-conscious he put his hand to his chin. The roughened skin reminded him that he hadn't shaved before showering.

'Did you want a ride to Atlanta House today?' It was kind of an apology. But most of him expected her to say no, sure she only did her 'charity bit' on the days when she had nothing better to do, or when there was bound to be an audience.

Her expression darkened. 'Yes, but—'

'I'll take you.'

'I can manage.'

'I'll take you.' He overrode her—pleased because she was going, pleased with himself because he'd got to her place just in time. 'Anything to carry this week?'

She jerked her head towards the black case by the door. He stepped forward, lifted his brows at the size of it.

'What's in that?' he asked, hefting the case from one hand to the other so he could hold the door.

'Just girl stuff.' She wouldn't look at him.

He wanted her to smile. 'Like what? Movies? Popcorn?'

'Pedicures actually.'

He paused. She looked at him then and he saw the flicker of amusement.

'When they get big, sometimes the girls can't reach their toes any more.'

It wasn't something he'd ever thought about before and he wasn't sure he wanted to again. 'So you're going to do it for them?' The picture of Liss on her knees polishing someone else's toenails seemed so unlikely he was about to laugh. Until he saw her defensively earnest expression.

'I might not be so good at organising paper files, James, but I'm pretty handy with a nail file.'

Reluctantly he acknowledged the admiration filling him. 'I never knew nail files were so heavy.'

The giggle suddenly bubbled out of her. It was such a nice sound and it shattered the heaviness between them.

'That would be the foot spa.' She giggled some more. 'Or maybe the jar of salts.'

'*Foot spa?*'

Her giggle became full-blown laughter and he found his slid easily from him too. She smiled at him then—just as he'd wanted her to. And all the bad feeling of the night disappeared.

'It is a bit ridiculous.' She looked rueful.

'No.' He shook his head at her, grinning widely. 'It's nice. It's a nice thing to do. My mother does a lot of charity work but I don't think she's ever clipped someone's toenails for them.'

'No? She's obviously not supporting the right ones.' Liss twinkled. 'What does she support?'

James shrugged, already regretting thinking of her, mentioning her. 'Whichever is flavour of the day.' The heaviness returned like a bad hangover.

Liss was looking expectant, waiting for more—all the way down in the lift.

'She's on a million committees.' He eventually broadened—briefly. But he couldn't hide the sarcastic undertone. 'She keeps busy. She likes to be seen to be active on that circuit.' Outward appearances were everything after all.

Liss kept pace with him to the car, pressed him right on the button. 'You're not close?'

He really regretted mentioning her. 'Not really.'

Not at all. It might have all fallen apart that day in his last year of school, when he'd come home early on a study break. His mother had come downstairs in a hurry. And then that guy had appeared—walking slowly, and so damn arrogantly down the stairs. She'd said he was there to talk about finances for one of her charities. And that needed to happen upstairs where the bedrooms were? What did they think he was, stupid?

He was conscious of Liss's intense scrutiny as he loaded her bag into the boot of the car. Finally he felt compelled to fill the silence she was making so obvious. So he shrugged again. 'You know. Mothers.'

He started the car. Hoped this bit of the conversation was over.

'No.' Liss shook her head. 'I wasn't close to either of my parents. We had a succession of nannies and then it was boarding school.'

James glanced at her, interest piqued. That must have been weird. Up until he'd discovered his mum's affair, life had been pretty sweet in his home, whereas Liss had always had it crazy. 'What about your sister?'

Her smile was soft. 'We're close. Different, but close. Kitty might be older but she's more vulnerable—she always has her nose in a book and her head in the clouds.'

Clearly Liss thought she was the more streetwise. James grinned. 'So you kept an eye out for her, huh?'

'Of course.'

So who kept an eye out for Liss, then? 'What about your brothers?'

'I'm not that close to them either.'

'Why is that?' Thinking about it he'd never heard Alex say much about his youngest sister. All he'd said was that she was unmanageable and he needed her off the island while the succession was sorted out. It struck James that Liss wasn't really that unmanageable at all. And as to the question as to who was more vulnerable—James thought maybe he should reserve judgment.

'Just different I guess.' She shrugged. 'I have some really great friends though.'

Did she? *Really?*

'What about your dad?' Liss turned the spotlight back on him. 'Are you close to him?'

James pressed a little harder on the accelerator. His mother had put a barrier between him and his father. In some ways he found that even more unforgivable. To tell, or not to tell? He'd been burdened with that dilemma for too long—until the day he'd found out he was just as stupid as his dad.

'More so in recent years.' Now he had more in common with his dad than he'd ever wanted. Learnt the hard way not to be so scathing of his father's blindness, and had developed some empathy.

He had to pull over then to let her out. He hoisted the case out of the boot and set it down for her. 'Have fun with all those toes.'

She flicked her fingers and he watched her go in. Her hair swung side to side in the simple ponytail as she wheeled her case behind her. If she was wearing make-up he couldn't tell. But, hell, she was beautiful.

He didn't go to work. He sat at a café, had three coffees and brooded, staring out the windows at the passers-by. He carefully avoided all the glossy mags stacked at the end of the counter. Having the moment his lover betrayed him with another man caught on film and printed in every magazine there was had put him off them. It wasn't an experience he wanted to repeat. Besides, he didn't want to see the all-glam Princess Elissa in them today; he'd rather see her as she was at this moment—fresh and relaxed.

When he pulled up at the house a couple of hours later they were all sitting on the veranda outside, legs outstretched—

drying toenails presumably. He smothered the chuckle. It was quite a sight.

'Liss, your boyfriend-bodyguard-boss is here.'

Liss rolled her eyes. 'Couple of weeks this time, girls.' And smiled away the chorus of disappointment.

The drive home was quick, she quietly chatted, told him a little about a couple of the girls. It wasn't until they were in the lift that he looked down and noticed her feet. Every toe was painted a different colour—an array of shimmer, gloss and matte.

'Like the rainbow look.' He winked.

She laughed. 'They wanted to see what they were like on so they could choose.'

He dropped to his knees. 'I like that one best.' He tweaked the crimson-tipped fourth toe on her left foot. Hell, even her toes were beautiful.

'Twist of Temptation. Good choice,' she said lightly and moved her foot away.

The lift doors opened as he stood, and then he noticed the pink splotches on her chest, saw the way her breathing had quickened. He moved, made the doors stay open by standing between them.

'Not going to reciprocate the coffee this week?' As if he needed more. He already had the shakes, or maybe that was just from the way she was wearing those jeans and the way she was so obviously affected.

'I...um...'

The pink tinges over her skin darkened and he fought hard to quell the urge to reach out and smooth across it, to trace down the path beneath the tee shirt and find out what other parts of her body were reddened. He badly wanted to touch, to taste, to...

'That's OK. You're right. It's not a good idea. Enjoy the rest of your weekend.' He spoke quickly, stepped back into the lift and jabbed at the 'close doors' button with a tightly clenched fist, before he did something he was sure to regret.

Liss's sense of anticipation as she got to work on Monday was at a ridiculous level. She couldn't wait to get on with the rest of the party plans and she hardly dared admit to herself how much she was looking forward to seeing James again. The drive to and from Atlanta House on Saturday had been such an eye-opener. Seeing him laugh like that, seeing him in those jeans, unshaven, relaxed—no distance, no disapproval, only warmth in those eyes. Sure, he'd got touchy when she'd asked about his parents, but for once that had only made him seem more human.

It had almost wiped out the hurt from his words of the night before. It almost made her wonder whether, if it weren't for the raging lust she felt for him, he'd make a great friend. Someone to laugh with, someone to listen to, someone to lean on. But the attraction between them meant a pure friendship was impossible. And it was clear he as much as she was working hard not to act on that attraction. She wondered why. And most of all, she wondered how long they could keep up the fight.

She'd only been at her desk for a few minutes before Katie came up to drop the papers in. She gave Liss a coy look. 'You and James looked like you were enjoying that art gallery do the other night.'

'You were there?'

Katie's laugh was more of a snort. 'Hardly.'

'Oh—'

'The picture in the paper—haven't you seen it?'

Liss shook her head, heart heading south. 'I don't tend to look.'

'You should—you're always in them, looking gorgeous.' The receptionist smiled again, but Liss worried that it didn't quite reach her eyes. 'The two of you looked pretty intense.'

She'd look at it in a moment—in private. She said nothing, already certain Katie's mind was going in directions Liss didn't want.

'How's the party planning going?' Katie asked. 'Lucky you getting to do that.'

It was a no-brainer to see where she was driving—just as Liss had expected. Her defences rose immediately. Great, Katie, and probably the rest of the staff, thought she'd got the fun job by having a fling with the boss. An open denial would be futile. Katie and the others would believe what they wanted to—Liss knew the truth was irrelevant. When it came to reputation versus reality, people always preferred the juicier option.

'I guess he asked me to do it because I know Aristo so well.'

'Yeah.' Katie's smile was sharp and her eyes full of scepticism. 'I guess.'

The second she'd gone, Liss rifled through the papers. The photo was of their profiles. She and James face to face. Full colour and, as Katie had said, intense. Eyes nowhere but on each other.

This was no way to keep speculation at bay and it made her even more determined to keep her distance. But she felt torn because, despite the words of Friday night, on Saturday they'd laughed together. Really laughed. And it had been so nice she wanted more. But already there was talk and she would not have all her hard work jeopardised. She wanted to succeed—*on her own* and have that achievement recognised. She was going to have to fight the attraction harder.

He still hadn't appeared by lunchtime. Mid-afternoon she phoned down to Katie. 'Do you know where James is?'

'In Melbourne,' came the slightly tart reply. 'Didn't you know?'

'No.' Liss hoped that her lack of knowledge of his trip might score her some points in the credibility stakes. Just so long as the sharp disappointment she'd felt hadn't registered in her voice. And she didn't want to ask when he was due back for fear Katie would misconstrue the interest.

The next few days sped in a flurry of organisation and mild panic. She fired an email to Cassie via Sebastian, giving her travel details. Cassie wasn't coming to the ball—with all the hoopla surrounding Sebastian's abdication the last thing they wanted was to be out at the mercy of the gossipy Aristan socialites. None of the others were going either—there was too much going on, with Alex on the hunt for the diamond and the succession so uncertain. Liss would be the only royal present. Liss understood why, but she would have loved to have had a friendly face there. And it would have been great to have someone see her success. But it wasn't to be. Hopefully she'd have time to meet up with Cassie in the days after.

So on she worked, finalising details, checking, double-checking that everything she'd planned would result in perfection. And as every day passed the anticipation, the adrenalin, built in her body—more and more, until finally she felt unable to sleep, unable to eat. She missed him. Every day she came into work hoping he'd be there, fighting the disappointment when he wasn't. Hope then built again—that he might appear during the day. She was turning into a scatter-brained mess and she had to find some method of release. Finally she fell back on her all-time favourite way of letting off steam—she'd go dancing.

* * *

After seeing the photo in the paper of the two of them at the art gallery, James delayed his return to Sydney until the afternoon before they were scheduled to fly to Aristo. He could no longer trust himself not to give into temptation and he didn't want to risk being recorded by some paparazzi. Getting snapped with her a second time would lead to serious speculation in the tabloids—they'd blow it way out of proportion. As it was he knew there'd be some questioning looks in his office. He told himself he could cope with that, but only on his terms—and privacy was one of them. The humiliation of Jenny's so very public betrayal had been enough. If they were to deal with this, they would, but no one would know. And until then, physical distance was the only answer.

Landing back in Sydney and getting to the office late, he found the staff had left for the day. But he knew he couldn't go another night without seeing her. He headed out to the usual nightspots—eventually finding her down on the dance floor of one of them.

He couldn't stop going nearer to her, watching her over the balcony area above. As she swayed to the relentless rhythm of the bass he tried to control his body's basic reaction. His jaw ached from clenching his teeth so hard. All he could think about was that kiss—where he'd been singed and his hands still hurt from not holding her. He badly wanted a repeat. He'd known it would be good. He hadn't known it would go ballistic. And he refused to believe it had been 'just' a kiss for her too. The way she looked at him, the awareness in her body, the way she flushed if he got too close—she was totally strung out.

Good. Because so was he.

He was sick of this heavy sense of foreboding. Desire was driving him now—his arms were empty and aching. The urge to haul her close was overwhelming and he knew he couldn't fight it any more.

He glanced around the room. Saw many others watching her too. She was dancing with a group of girls—all of them attractive, but it was Liss that the crowd was watching, the one who many were wanting.

He knew what he was getting himself into. He wouldn't invest any emotion. It would be purely physical. It wouldn't take much to make the flame burn out. A fast and furious glow and it would be over.

It was different from Jenny because this time he had his eyes wide open. He already knew not to trust Liss. She wasn't about to be hurt—she'd find some other beau before James would have the chance to blink. He gritted his teeth harder at the wave of rage that rose with that thought. Damn it, he had to control that. And he decided the only way was to give her an experience *she'd* never forget—make sure it was so damn good she'd be ruined for the next guy. Because there would be a next guy. It was only a matter of time. For women like Liss, one lover would never be enough.

He watched her dance for another moment, but couldn't take it any more. He walked out without saying hello to anyone.

They were flying out to Aristo tomorrow. Just the two of them. There would be no observers, no paparazzi on the plane. Just him, just her. And it was time to fight the fire with fire.

CHAPTER SEVEN

'LATE night, Liss?'

Hiding behind her large dark glasses, she took the hint of disapproval on the chin. After her nil response they rode to the airport in silence but the atmosphere was thick with swirling heat. She stared out the window, not able to cope with seeing James as well as having him up close in the back of the taxi. He was looking too gorgeous in a white cotton tee that wasn't too tight, but tight enough to show off that broad chest and long arms, jeans that were a relaxed fit but with enough shape to make her appreciate the length of his legs and the hint of their concealed power. She badly, badly wanted to touch.

They cruised through check-in and waited in the club lounge for a few minutes before getting the call to board. She gripped her small flight bag and walked ahead so she wouldn't have to see any longer how well he filled out those jeans.

She'd danced and danced on into the night—needing to burn the energy. Now she was tired and strung out and he wasn't helping because every time she glanced at him he met her gaze with a smile that set her every cell singing.

She stepped into the cabin with relief. First class wasn't

usually fully booked and she planned to stretch out and enjoy the space. She fussed about, unloading a few essentials from her bag into the compartment by her seat: her own water, her warm wool socks, her vial of refreshingly scented oil—the little things she needed to make the journey as relaxing as possible. Then she realised that James was standing right behind her, patiently watching, waiting—for what? She raised her brows—hoping it looked like a cool question.

He flashed the charm smile. 'Actually the window seat is mine.'

She checked her ticket quickly. Damn. Her consternation must have been obvious because his smile widened with wicked humour.

'Don't you want to sit next to me?'

The flush flooded her—she could feel it all the way from her face to her toes, and she wondered how he'd react if she answered honestly. She wanted to sit *on* him, not next to him. She wanted to straddle his strong, heavy thighs—to feel the muscle-filled denim on her bare skin. She wanted to slide her fingers beneath that white tee shirt and feel for herself the heat of his chest—was it hair-tickled or smooth? Was it as bronzed as his arms or was it paler, less kissed by the sun…? *Kissed*…oh, hell, she was in trouble.

'But you can have the window if you like.' The lights in his eyes were brightening, the smile widening.

'You're sure?' She couldn't look away from him, couldn't stop sounding like a breathless temp offered the long-term placement of a lifetime.

'I've already got a beautiful view.'

OK. Deep breath—and time to get a grip on the situation. She stayed standing.

'Take it.'

'You're the boss,' she said, to remind herself as much as anything.

'And you're the princess,' he said. 'Interesting power play, isn't it? Who do you think should be on top?'

She sat in an awful hurry. On top? He wanted to debate *positions?* She tried to think of a witty reply—hell, any sort of reply. 'You said my being a princess wouldn't garner me any special treatment.'

'Right.' He sat next to her and leaned close, continuing with the chatty tone that softened the underlying determined quality. 'And just because I'm the boss doesn't mean I should get any either. Not in this arena.'

'What arena's that?' He was all she could see—his large body screened the rest of the cabin from her. It was as if they were in their own little corner of the plane and he was shielding her from all observers.

'The personal one.'

'We're talking personal?'

'Come on, princess, we've barely talked anything else.' His eyes held hers, daring her to be honest. 'Have we?'

She paused, looked down as she clicked her safety belt in place. 'You're the one who said it's not a good idea, James.'

'You said it too. And we're both right. It's probably really stupid.' He tilted her chin with his fingers, making her look at him again, making her active in the conversation, making her skin sizzle. 'But it also seems to be impossible to ignore.'

His touch both soothed and rasped over her stretched nerves. She moved her head enough to make him release her, but maintained the eye contact—she had the feeling he wouldn't settle for less.

'So,' he muttered. 'Let's talk personal.'

The engines of the plane revved and she felt the situation

slipping from her control. She fought to reclaim it. 'Are you sure this is the right place?'

'Why not?' The glints in his eye spiked. 'We have a number of hours to fill in. What else do you suggest we do?'

They stared at each other and in the darkness of his eyes she saw all her wild fantasies reflected—of closeness and warmth, of sighs and the sound of them slipping together, of naked sensation. Until finally she ducked away from his gaze in heated defeat, closing her eyes as the plane gained enough speed to lift off from the ground.

It was only when the plane levelled out high in the sky, that she expelled the breath she'd been holding and replied, 'Talking is good.'

She couldn't join him as he chuckled. This wasn't that funny for her—it was full on. But OK. He wanted to talk personal? Maybe she'd take the opportunity to do some digging—she had a few questions she'd like answered. 'Do you ever really have a good time, James?'

He sobered instantly and placed his hand over hers. She had to concentrate extra hard to listen for the answer and not let her brain go fuzzy from the body contact.

'What do you mean by that?' He sounded surprised.

'You're never really in the gossip pages of the papers or magazines—even though your family is almost as well known in Sydney as mine is on Aristo. And sometimes you don't look like you're having so much fun.'

'How do I look?'

She thought for a moment and then opted for the truth. 'Intense.' And definitely brooding. There had been times when she'd seen the serious look descend over the charming features and she figured he was thinking about something—some sort of bother. Was it work or was it a woman?

His voice was low and gently mocked. 'I know how to have a good time, princess.' He shot her a look that made her more than aware of the kind of fun he was thinking of right now.

Fantasies of dark nights swirled in her head once more.

'Just because you like to party on the pages of the gossip magazines doesn't mean the rest of us have to. I don't need publicity to prove what a good time I'm having.' His fingers tightened, stopping her from withdrawing her hand. 'I prefer to keep my wild times private, not have them dissected in the papers.'

That one really rankled. It was one thing that her brothers really frowned on. It had been OK for them to get up to whatever in the good old days, but the minute there was wind of a story on her they came down hard. She curled her fingers away from his.

'You shouldn't believe everything you read.'

His expression darkened. 'Really?' He smoothed the palm of his hand along the ridge of her fist.

Liss watched as exactly the intense brooding look she'd meant descended on his features. Then she watched him take a deliberately deep breath, visibly aiming to relax. 'Actually, I've been wondering about one salacious detail for some time.'

She raised a brow and tried to look as if she didn't care that much. The papers wrote an awful lot of rubbish—recycled pictures and added tired old quotes from people she'd never met.

He leaned towards her, voice lowered. 'Whether it's true you usually go without underwear in your trademark slinky party dresses.'

She couldn't help the smile at that, a bubble of laughter stirred and her flirt mood revived. 'That's for me to know.'

She couldn't resist throwing him the challenge. 'Think you're going to find out?'

'I'd be willing to bet on it.' He shot the answer straight back.

It *almost* stopped her—but not quite. 'I'm not a betting woman.'

'Wise girl. In your shoes I wouldn't be either.' He grinned wickedly, reminding her of their race the other week. 'Who'd be fool enough to bet against a dead certainty?'

She tried to think of something suitably cutting to say only her brain wasn't working as fast as it usually did. 'You're very confident.'

'I am,' he agreed softly. 'Want to know why?'

He lifted his hand from hers, took a pinch of her hair and tugged so she turned her head his way again. One look into those eyes again and she was mesmerised.

Utterly still she sat as he drew closer, blocking everything from her senses but him.

'This is why,' he muttered. He let go of her hair, but his hand didn't leave her head. His fingers slipped down the side of her face, and he traced around the curve of her jaw. The smallest touch was sensational—it was as if tiny fireworks had been set off along his path and the next patch of skin demanded its share…but most especially it was her mouth that wanted his attention. She had to open it, just a little. She had…to…*breathe*. The small creases at the corners of his eyes deepened a fraction. He knew. And then he responded—his finger traced up from her chin and slowly, with delicate pressure, he rubbed the tip of it back and forth over her lips. They felt dry and full and needy. What she'd give for a drink right now—a drink straight from his mouth.

His slow, delicious, tormenting caresses didn't stop. Just one finger, cruising the contours of her lips and she couldn't look away from the promise of passion in his eyes. She forgot where they were, the low hum of the airplane faded to nothing—only conscious of the sound of her own breathing and the intensity of his attention.

To her equal dismay and pleasure he moved his finger from her mouth, running it down the length of her throat, circling around the hollow at the base of it. Then he slid it first one side, then the other, to smooth over her collarbones.

She wanted to say something, but couldn't think what. Couldn't think at all. His gaze dropped, breaking the stare, and the corners of his mouth lifted into that smile that she half loathed, half loved. And his finger went lower, right down the centre of her breastbone. He flicked to one side and with slow deliberation circled around her nipple.

'This is why,' he repeated softly.

She looked down and discovered a bra wasn't necessary when James paid attention to her breasts. He had a better effect than any support or surgery ever could. She could feel the way they'd swollen and lifted, tightening at his touch. Now, in her thin top, her nipples were clearly visible—peaks jutting out, begging for attention. They were so hard it hurt.

She looked back at his sardonic expression and realised that he was still in control. While only the slightest of touches had had her almost on her knees wanting more, he was sitting back—the amused antagonist. She wanted him to be as affected as she was.

She pushed his hand away and sat up sharply. 'It's the air-conditioning.' She inserted as much frost as possible into her reply. 'Planes. I'm always cold on them.'

His laugh was warm and inside she softened in response. She responded the way she did to everything he did—uncontrollably.

'Really?' he teased. 'Then why are you so hot here?' His fingers traipsed leisurely across her brow. His voice dropped even lower, a lover's whisper. 'Where else are you hot, princess?'

She stared into eyes that were dark and devastating. She knew she was sinking into them. Her body melting; if he kissed her again she'd lose it.

The sexual attraction was like a third force—there was her, there was him, and there was this thing between them— drawing her closer, ever closer.

And she was hot everywhere. Was it the same for him? Couldn't be—or he wouldn't have been able to stop so easily last time.

James was making a claim. But he wasn't relinquishing control—not of himself or of the situation. It made him a challenge she wasn't sure she had the strength to pass on.

But he *was* her boss. And there was something else about James that put her even more on alert. Partly, it was the sheer strength of that physical attraction, but partly it was because she had the feeling he'd see right through her if she let him.

What would he see? Anything? It was strangely important to her that he think well of her. Stupid, when so few people in authority like him did. So, for now, she'd retreat. Laugh the whole thing off with some sarcasm. 'Do you always try to sleep with your secretaries?'

He sat back, obviously amused. 'Only the ones above average height, with dark hair and who aren't afraid to bite back.'

She pretended to think for a bit. 'Maria in Accounts would suit.'

'Maria in Accounts has a husband and two children. That would be messy. I never do messy.'

'Really? What do you do, then?'

'Start it simple, keep it physical, end it clean and final.'

She bit the inside of her cheek. That was honesty from him, then—short and to the point and now she knew where she stood. 'And you're thinking of starting it with me?'

'Sweetheart, you know we've already started.'

Yeah, but it didn't seem that simple to her.

'It is going to happen, you know.' His eyes were lasers—truth seekers.

'That certain bet?'

'Dead certain—remember?' He nodded slowly. 'I've finally accepted that.'

'Gosh, you sound so thrilled about it,' she said with faux jollity, stung by the comment. Then she glared. 'It's not like you're the only one with the decision to make.'

'Don't tell me you haven't already decided.'

Her jaw dropped at that.

'I'm not being arrogant.' He pushed her chin back up. 'I'm being honest.' He didn't look that happy about it. 'Besides, it's a little bigger than the both of us, isn't it?' He spoke lightly, his eyes roaming over her mouth. 'The want.'

Her lips could almost feel the caresses from his gaze. It took a moment for her to hear his next softly spoken words.

'And you've been a little cautious about it too, haven't you?'

Of course.

Then he offered a solution for both of them. 'If we give in to it, it will go away.'

Her chest tightened. So he wanted it to go away. He didn't want to be attracted to her. But he was—just as she was attracted to him. He wanted to work it through and be rid of it.

She suppressed the shiver that ran through her body—a mix of desire and of despair.

He unclipped his safety belt, got a couple of soft wool blankets from the locker and sat again. Reached across and unclipped her belt too.

'Let's get you comfortable, hmm?' He spread one blanket out over her and the other over himself. The two overlapped. 'Can't have you getting *cold*.' He smiled, oblivious to the mix of hurt and heat she felt inside.

But as he drew closer it was the heat that spread, the desire to have him even closer still. His eyes were huge and seemed to read hers, seemed to know exactly what she was thinking— because they reflected it.

'You warm enough?' It was a whisper, spoken as his lips lowered. Still not quite close enough. And she was so focused on them, on willing them nearer, that she couldn't manage to give the answer that was undoubtedly obvious anyway.

'Princess?'

She lifted her chin and tasted his smile as she pressed her lips to his.

She meant to play it cool. She meant to stay in control. She meant to hide just how hot she was—how hot she thought he was—and try to find out how affected *he* was. But her mouth parted hungrily without her consent. Welcoming his wickedly teasing tongue once more, wanting him to work it the way he had the other day—and then some. His hands were firm on her jaw, fingers spread, holding her face up to his. Broad palms and long fingers meant he easily cupped her chin and sent fingers down the length of her throat. In a second the kiss was hot and deep and she was shaking with the joy of having him back inside—she wanted more of him inside.

Too soon he lifted his head. He studied her. She couldn't hide the way her breathing was fast and out of kilter.

'Not getting too excited, there, are you, princess?' he said, half-smile in place. 'It was just a kiss.'

Nothing of the sort. He knew it. She knew it. He was just proving how hollow her words of the other night had been. But he couldn't blame a woman for wanting to salvage a little pride, could he? Not when he'd been the one to freeze over faster than a raindrop in Antarctica.

Suddenly she feared that being with James could somehow strip her of all pride—and dignity. But just as the fear sent a chill through her, he banished it, simply by taking her mouth again in a lightning-fast move. She was breathless, her slim control toppled completely. She lifted her hands to his head, feeling his hair beneath her fingers. Eyes closing, she let touch and taste and scent envelop her. Shifting in her seat, wanting to move, wanting to moan.

'Settle down, sweetheart.' He lifted his mouth from hers again and stroked hands down her arms in a way she knew he intended to be soothing, not stirring. She was still stirred. He spoke some more. 'I'm not having quick sex in some tiny toilet, even if it is first class.'

What? The sex or the toilet? Oh, she knew the sex would be beyond first class—if his kiss was anything to go by, it would be the best of her life.

She sucked in three lungs full of air and used the extra to clear her head enough to be able to come back with a sort of smart reply. She had to try to handle him and the only way seemed to be to keep it light—or at least try to. 'Hell, no. Too small, too smelly.'

'If we're going to do it we're going to do it properly.'

'Hallelujah,' she quipped, only half joking.

He sort of smiled but his delivery was soft and serious. 'It'll be slow, in a bed, with plenty of space, and no one nearby so you can scream away.'

She suppressed the thrill of the image and aimed for cool and sarcastic. 'What makes you so sure I'll be screaming?' It was too breathy to be believable.

His eyes held hers and told her to quit trying to hide it. 'I won't stop until you do.'

CHAPTER EIGHT

Liss stood no chance. Her mind was spinning. James Black on flirt offensive? With his playful side unleashed, he was far more dangerous than when in lecturing-boss-man mode. He'd made his decision and now was embarking on a slow, deliberate assault. And she was about to cave. It was too exciting not to, too much of a temptation not to, too much of a need not to.

Under the blanket his fingers touched her breast. She shivered as her nipple tightened even harder.

'Damn air-conditioning,' he murmured and pulled the blankets higher—to their necks. Then his fingers went to play some more.

'James,' she warned.

'What? All I'm trying to do is warm you up a little, princess. You've gone all taut and goose bumpy.'

She was only going to go even more taut the way he was working her. 'James. I will retaliate.'

His hot laughter on her neck only turned her on more. 'I'd like to see you try.'

'You don't know who you're playing with.' Bravado all the way—and how she was aching for him to take her all the way.

'Go on, then. Try me.'

She turned more towards him, got as close as the damn airline seats would allow, and slid her fingers under his tee— just as she'd dreamed of doing in the departure lounge. She smoothed palms across his chest, exploring the breadth and warmth. Then, impatient as always, she slid them lower, tracking down the arrow of hair that felt slightly rough beneath her fingertips. To the belt of his jeans. It was surprisingly easy to push the tongue of the belt through the loop one-handed, without being able to see it under the blanket.

His breathing deepened.

But there was no way she could get the fly of his jeans undone—it was pulled too taut by the straining ridge beneath. She had to be content with stroking the length of it—up and down through the material. Quite desperately she wanted to feel him bare in her hand. She'd take him in her mouth if she thought she could get away with it, if they could somehow be discreet.

He must have read her mind because he looked into her eyes, his own slightly glassy. And his hand moved under the blanket, covering hers, not gripping harshly but firm enough to stop her from her task.

'I can't let you do that.'

'Why not?' she muttered, excited by the feel of him, the thick length. She wanted him free, right up against his stomach, and she really wished she could take a good look because it felt fantastic—big and hard.

'You know what you're doing to me, don't you?'

'I think so.' She smiled.

And then he smiled back at her—a smile of warmth and want and no hint of mockery or sarcasm. And while she was melting he stole the advantage back.

He easily gripped both her hands in one of his, dragging her half across the seat and almost into his own. He angled her so her shoulder and upper back rested on his chest, so they were both looking towards the windows. Then, under cover of the blankets, he slipped his fingers under her top, pushed aside the lace of her bra and teased her nipple. He nuzzled her neck and she closed her eyes—wanting, wanting, wanting *more*.

He knew. He moved, worked his hand down the front of her pants, easily slipping between fabric and skin. They didn't kiss again, not wanting to draw attention from other passengers—not wanting the intensity broken. Instead his hand moved, with almost imperceptible movements—tiny rubbing ones, which she matched with tiny rocking. And his other hand held both of hers and she felt bound to him, to the sensual spell he had her under. He was leading the dance and she seemed to have no option but to follow. There was no escape; she could only ride on the storm he was brewing.

Suddenly the inevitability of it oppressed her and she filled with the need to fight, to gain some control over her raging desires, some control over him.

She clamped her upper thighs together. 'I'm not going to have an orgasm on an aeroplane surrounded by passengers.' She choked the words out.

'No?' His voice was rough. 'But you're close.' Statement not question.

His breath stirred her ear and she closed her eyes, pressing her lips tighter together, trying to stop the moans, trying to stop the sensations from overwhelming her. How could she want him so badly?

'You really are built for pleasure, aren't you?'

Something in the way he said it made her freeze completely. What was she doing having a grope in public? This was a cheap and easy thrill—was that all he thought she was? What about *him*?

'James. Stop.'

He did immediately. Got the ice in her tone and got his hand out of her pants. She turned. His frown was almost imperceptible but it was there.

'And here was me thinking you were a wild child,' he said. 'A hedonist. Someone who'd take pleasure any chance she could get it.'

She moved, going to the far side of her own seat—putting what little distance she could between them. 'I'm not everything you think me, James.' She smiled and bluffed. 'It has to be the right place, the right time.' She paused. 'The right person.'

'The right person, for the right moment.'

Momentary. She rebelled against his automatic assumption that this would be short-lived. Why did everyone think anything she was involved in would be transient?

But his attention was still on her body. 'What will you be like? Will you close your eyes or will you let me see you raw in your ecstasy?'

'You're wondering what kind of performance you'll get?' Her frustration moved to anger.

His eyes lifted, trapping hers, and it was all serious intensity. 'I'm not interested in *performance*. I'm not interested in the princess thing or anything of the trappings. I'm interested in what's underneath.'

She knew he didn't mean her clothes. 'What if there's nothing?'

That stopped him. Their eyes met—stripped of desire, forced to reveal painful honesty.

He spoke, the words ground out slowly as he frowned. 'I don't want to believe that.' He reached his hand across the seats and spread his fingers slightly to the left of her breastbone. The palm of his hand pressed against her heart. His hand was big and strong and she knew he could hold her heart in that one hand alone. The thought was scary.

He pushed, fingers digging a little into her breast as he emphasised his words. 'I'd like to think there might be things in there that you don't let anyone see.'

'Why, James.' She laughed, wanting to push him back, not wanting him to feel how much faster her heart beat when he touched her, when he pried too close. 'You're a romantic.'

The momentary openness in his gaze was shuttered. His hand withdrew. 'I'm not, princess. I've already told you the way I play it. So don't delude yourself about me. You do enough of that in other areas of your life already.'

It was OK for him to challenge her, but not for her to question him? All she wanted was the same as what he wanted from her—to find out what was underneath. Yes, he was charming and witty and urbane, but not very far under the surface was this layer of steel that hid a depth to his personality. She wanted to understand why he kept it so reserved. But he wasn't going to let her. So why should she grant him things that he wasn't about to give her?

She knew he wanted her. But she also knew he didn't want to. And while she knew the reasons why an affair with him was a bad idea for her, she didn't know his reasons. Couldn't understand why he didn't want to want her so badly. She didn't quite know how to respond to that.

All the heat faded and she truly did feel cold.

He draped his blanket on top of hers, giving her the extra layer. 'You should get some rest. You've got a big night ahead of you tomorrow.'

She felt the finality of his words and got the message. The fooling around was finished. Light, naughty talk was all it was—he might have said he wanted to see what was beneath her surface, but it was just words. He certainly didn't see her real self, not right now—and she'd never be able to show him. Not when she knew he wasn't interested in anything more than burning out the flame.

But she still wanted him. And if she was going to have him, then she would make sure he was a slave to it as much as she was.

When they finally arrived on Aristo it was early on the morning of the party. James headed straight into meetings with the contractors and Liss buzzed straight to the ballroom to make sure all the plans were in place. The catering company had use of the kitchen and she was pleased to see all the food had arrived and was being prepared with the finishing touches she'd requested.

With a satisfied air she watched for a while as the army of florists worked. The building itself was spectacular. She'd just added some exquisite details. There was no way it wouldn't be a success.

In the late afternoon she dressed with care but with speed, hyped on adrenalin. Underneath she bubbled with the kind of excitement that came only from anticipation of what delights the evening might bring. The evening when James would be wearing a tux and, fingers crossed, be totally wowed by all her efforts. Surely, once the party was done, she deserved a little reward? Technically her work for him would be done, so she could kind of argue that he was no longer her boss. And no one else from the Sydney office was here. No one would know…

She paused in the doorway, the earliest she'd ever arrived at a ball, but as she was effectively the hostess she had to be here to greet her guests. She ran her hands over her hips—smoothing the sensuous fabric with satisfaction. She'd gone

with black—classic, elegant. A one-off designer number—
sexy and sophisticated, and she'd been saving it for just such
an occasion.

James saw her immediately; for a moment they looked
each other over and the electric attraction pulsed between
them. The flash of heat was so intense she wanted to bail out
on the ball and have him in her room right then. Nobody, but
nobody wore a tux the way James Black did.

'Princess.' He was the one who spoke, reminding her of
the presence of the manager, of all the wait staff.

'You've done a wonderful job with the decoration of the
ballroom,' the manager gushed.

Liss smiled, replied politely and wondered why James
wasn't gushing—he should be. But he stood quiet beside her
and then the guests began to arrive. As fun as it was catching
up with everyone she only had an awareness of him. Almost
on auto she mingled and mixed up the people, kept an eye
on the overview, ensuring everything was going as smoothly
as possible.

Waiters filled glasses from a fountain she'd had installed—it ceaselessly flowed with Cristal champagne. The
room was filled with the heady scent of the orchids she'd
had flown in specially. Gathered in large boughs, they were
exotic and dramatic and doused the place in an atmosphere
of expense.

She couldn't help frequently glancing at James to assess
his reaction. She saw him take some of the caviar that was
being offered on exquisite napkins. There was nothing more
exclusive. He ate one sample but didn't take another. She saw
him looking round at the guests filling the room, saw him look
at his watch. She felt pleased. They were all here, already—
all eager to come to what was the ball of the year. The dresses

and skin on show were something. She stood and smiled and chatted. A success, right from the start. She'd actually done it. A giddy glow warmed her—heightened by the knowledge that he was so close.

They weren't even an hour into it when James discreetly gestured for her to join him. She fell into step, her body tightening, teased by the thought of being alone with him. He led her out of the ballroom to one of the little meeting rooms down the corridor.

He waited for her to go in ahead of him. 'How do you think it's going?'

She smiled as she heard him close the door behind them and her level of excitement rose another notch. 'It's marvelous, isn't it?'

She looked at him and lost her smile immediately at the hard glare in his eyes. What? What was wrong?

'You don't think there's anything missing?'

She couldn't think of anything. Incredible food, incredible wine, incredible company—what else was there?

He nodded at her blankness. 'Why are we having this ball, princess?'

She really didn't like the way he said 'princess'. 'To celebrate the opening of the hotel.'

'Right. Why else?'

There was another reason for the celebration?

'To promote it, right?' He spoon-fed her the answer.

'Yes.' And it was a wonderful promotion—everyone would see how fabulous the hotel was.

'So what's missing?'

She really couldn't think—everyone who was anyone was here.

His temper started to show then as slowly, super sarcastically, he spelt it out for her. 'What about cameras, princess? Photographers. Journalists. TV people.'

Oh…

'This wasn't just some jolly for you to arrange for all your mates, Elissa. I'm running a business here. I wanted it in every glossy magazine on the planet. Remember?'

Yes. That bit was coming back to her now.

'You didn't arrange flights and accommodation for any press, did you?'

Feeling too sick to speak, she simply shook her head. She'd been too busy planning all the exclusive stuff and inviting the who's who.

'What did you think was going to happen—that the world's media would flock just because *you're* in attendance? Well, sorry, sweetheart, this wasn't about some blurry paparazzi shot showing you worse for wear.'

The words knifed deep into her heart.

'It isn't all about you, princess.'

The knife twisted.

'I just can't believe you could screw this up. What on earth were you thinking?'

She'd been thinking of him.

'When I ask you to do a job, you do it—*properly.*'

She'd tried, she'd really tried but…

'It's my own fault.' He spoke more to himself than her. 'I should never have left this up to you. I should never have thought for a second that you could manage it.'

She had no answer to that.

He pressed his fingers to his temples, visibly trying to contain his temper. She'd really rather he yelled and stomped around the room a bit. But he was too much of a man for that—with too good a rein on his emotions.

And it really hurt. She stood still, not wanting to move, not wanting to breathe in case he flared and said something else in that horrible way. And she couldn't think of a thing to do to make it better.

'The champagne is good,' he finally spoke again—quiet, colourless.

She nodded, hoping for a lightening of the atmosphere. No way could he find fault with her taste. 'Cristal.'

'And the decoration on the napkins for the caviar— what's that?'

'Real gold leaf.' She managed to get her voice higher than a thread that time.

He grunted. Maybe it was a snort. Either way it didn't sound positive. 'So tell me.'

Tell him what? Hell, this was such a nightmare and he was stringing it out.

'How much?' he asked, as if it were obvious.

'Pardon?'

'How much did this party cost me?'

'Um.' She didn't want to admit she hadn't got all the bills and receipts together yet. In truth she didn't know what most of them would be.

'Do you even know what the budget for this was?'

Budget? Oh, right. There had been a spreadsheet in the file James had mentioned. She hadn't really got round to studying it. 'I didn't—'

'What, *think*?'

Damn it, she'd done nothing but think about this party. 'You said you wanted the *best*.'

'You have no idea, do you, princess? A modern-day Marie Antoinette—utterly clueless.'

'James, I…' have no idea what to say.

'Good thing I'm a wealthy man and can carry the blow.' He looked, his eyes skimming over her, all dreaded sarcasm and nil humour. 'You seriously need to grow up, Elissa.'

She bit hard on the inside of her lip. She'd heard that one before—from her father, from her brothers. But it was different this time.

She was not going to cry. Not going to. Not going to act like the spoilt, sulky girl he thought she was. She'd take the caning like a professional. And cry later.

He was serious. And she knew it was all over. This wasn't something she could laugh off with a flippant comment. And for once she didn't want to. She felt terrible. She'd let him down. She'd let herself down.

She really was a waste of space.

'I'm sorry, James.'

He stared at her, definitely no forgiveness or ease in those hard, dark eyes. No sign of the golden lights. He didn't reply, just stalked out of the room.

CHAPTER NINE

JAMES practised a relaxed smile all the short walk back to the ballroom. Failed. Knew he was snarl central. He stopped just outside the room and took in a deep breath. A drink. That'd help. He collared a waiter. The expensive bubbles hit the spot but didn't soothe quite the way he wanted. He could feel the steam coming out of his ears. It wasn't just the wasted opportunity for coverage that had him riled. It was her—if anything he was even madder because she'd been so close to succeeding. He looked around. It was one damn impressive party. From the guest list, to the catering, she had arranged the best for the best.

And yet she'd forgotten the basics. He wanted to shake her.

She arrived back in the ballroom a few minutes after him. Looked a little flushed, headed to the other side of the room—soon in conversation with several guests.

He looked away then. Got to working some guests too—there was much that could be salvaged from the evening and he might as well get something out of it. A few hours passed and he steered well clear of her, knowing both his temper and temperature would stay cooking on high if he saw too much of her.

But she wouldn't leave his mind—and his frustration rumbled.

Eventually he caught sight of her quietly discussing something with one of the waiters. Angry as he was with her, he didn't like to see her so subdued. The sparkle had gone. The smile was still there but he could see the hint of strain. The flush had faded; now she was pale.

If only she'd made the media arrangements. It would have been a perfect night. She would have been so thrilled—and rightly so. He'd wanted her to taste that satisfaction, to know she'd done a good job and was capable of success.

Then he'd wanted to see her satisfied in a whole other, deeply personal, deeply physical, way.

He still wanted both to happen.

He didn't like that it wasn't going to be tonight.

Damn it, despite everything he still wanted to rip the dress from her and feel her warm and naked against him. Why did she have to be so bloody attractive?

He took a stroll about the room, trying to get to simmer level and not still be on rapid boil. But there was only one way to rid himself of this energy.

Unable to resist, he looked again. Now she was talking with some guests. She was aware of his scrutiny; he could tell by the way she stiffened slightly. But she wouldn't look him in the eye. He didn't like that either.

Time to work out solutions to both problems.

Would there never be an end to this hideous nightmare? All around her beautiful people ate beautiful food, had fabulous conversations and partied while inside Liss felt as alive as petrified wood.

She talked to a few local socialites, all wanting to regale her with all the gossip, and wanting to get more from her—about Cassie and Sebastian's relationship especially. Liss clammed up—Cassie and her brother had a right to privacy, had been through enough already. And the mention of Cassie's name only made her feel worse. She still hadn't been able to see her.

They asked about Sydney—and she found she couldn't share much about that either. As they were getting nothing from her, the women's conversation strayed onto royal affairs—literally.

'You've heard the latest one—that your father had an affair with a palace maid?' one beauty asked rather gleefully.

Her father, King Aegeus. The uncomfortable lump in her chest expanded. She'd hardly known him—the only times he'd shown interest in her in recent years was when he'd expressed his displeasure at her pursuits. She'd genuinely grieved at his death—for the relationship that *could* have been as much as for the life that had passed. She knew she'd missed out. He'd missed out too.

This new rumour annoyed her—maybe she got the gene for inappropriate lust from him. And the tales the women were telling only reminded her that tonight the dirt-dishing media wolves weren't here, and they should be.

'You shouldn't believe everything you hear,' Liss snapped. 'You should know that.'

There was a momentary silence, which Liss filled by simply having a long sip of her champagne. Not that it helped.

'Is that your boss?' one woman asked, looking over to Liss's right. 'Wow. He looks intense.'

'He looks hot,' said another.

Liss knew he was looking their way but she refused to look back. Instead she punished herself more by answering, 'Yes. And he's single. Why not go introduce yourselves?'

Slowly, after several long hours, the guests left. At last she could sneak away and shrivel up in peace.

Or not. As she made her way to the door James called her to him, the first time he'd spoken to her since he'd torn strips off her. Bracing herself, she walked over, looked into his darkly handsome face. To her surprise he was actually smiling. 'It's well after midnight. Going to start emptying those bottles now?'

And fire up her inner 'wild child'? Not now, possibly never again. But she wasn't going to show him how much tonight had affected her.

'Maybe a few, yes.' All bravado again. Maybe she should have a few dozen. Get blotto and wipe out all memory of this cursed night. But she knew it wouldn't work. She'd never forget this nightmare.

'Come finish one with me, then.'

Surely he was kidding? But he picked up a couple of glasses from a waiter and lifted, not a half-empty one, but a whole bottle of champagne. Carrying the lot in one large hand, he took her arm with his other and she pretty much had no choice but to walk the way he guided.

'Right.' She choked. 'Why not?' Her smile was half strangled and she felt like the damned going to dine with the executioner.

They left the ballroom—now almost empty except for waiting staff starting the big clean-up. Her heels sank a little on the thickly carpeted hallway. And even though the elevator whisked them up to the top floor with incredible smoothness, her stomach felt as if she'd been on an extreme roller coaster. And in the silence her heart beat louder than twenty drums in a marching band. And to make it all worse she felt dangerously close to tears.

He swiped his key card and ushered her into the penthouse suite. Gleaming marble tiles led to a kitchen, to a bathroom. Other doors must lead to bedrooms.

In the large lounge he'd set up office and it was to the desk that he headed, setting the glasses down and filling them. He held one out to her. She took a sip and he left his on the desk. 'So.'

She clutched the glass, stepped back and tried not to stare as he shrugged out of his jacket and put his shoulders even more on display in the fine white shirt. 'I won't bother coming back to Sydney with you. I can have my stuff packed and shipped.'

He leaned back on the desk, legs stretching out long in front of him. 'Are you resigning?'

'I thought it was too late for that.'

'I haven't fired you, princess. Not yet.'

'Oh.' What on earth was she going to do for him now? Be the tea lady? It would only take one hour of that occupation before he'd turf her out of it. Hell, she couldn't even make a decent coffee.

He wouldn't take his eyes off her. 'You blew the budget, you failed to invite half the necessary people, you totally screwed up the point of the party, but other than that it was an OK night.'

The vague compliment tacked onto the litany of failures got to her. An OK night? *OK?* For everyone else in that room it had been brilliant. And he knew it. Her defence mechanisms slowly started to crank up.

'I'll give you one last chance.'

She didn't know whether to be pleased or to laugh in his face. 'Last chance?' Didn't he get it yet? She'd failed. She was never going to 'get' this.

His stance looked indolent but his eyes were intent. 'Do it again.'

'Pardon?' She just wasn't following his conversation.

'I want another party. Bigger, better. With everyone we need here.'

Her attention snapped to his words.

'You have a quarter of the original budget and one week to do it.'

Another party? Another gala ball with all those people plus the media? With no money? 'You're kidding.'

'That's what I want. That's what you'll do.'

'I can't do it. Do you know how hard it was to get all those flowers shipped here? I can't repeat any of it. Most of the guests will be the same. They'll expect different. They'll expect *more*.'

'You better come up with something else, then, hadn't you? Something better. Something cheaper. Something quick.'

She stared. The full reality of what he was asking hit her. 'I can't,' she whispered.

He stood, drawing up to his full height, and walked nearer. 'I didn't think you'd be one to turn down a challenge, princess.'

There were challenges and there was asking the impossible.

But as he came closer her body tightened, and her fighting spirit returned. Maybe it was the rush of adrenalin at his proximity, but suddenly she was sick of his escalating demands. Tonight had been a good party; he could at least admit that.

'I know you can do this.' He put his hands on her shoulders. 'You can, Elissa.'

It was those softly spoken words, and his rare use of her name, that really got her back up.

'I'm not a child, James. You don't need to jolly me into it.' She shrugged her shoulders and his hands lifted off. Determined to get at least some credit from him, she went into battle mode. 'Tonight was a success. So I screwed up a couple of things. But it was still a damn good party.'

He said nothing and she rallied to press the point. 'The food was incredible.'

'It was.'

Wow. A concession. She pushed for another. 'The ballroom looked amazing.'

'It did.'

'The guests were all A-list.'

'They were.'

'The champagne fountain was just awesome.'

'It was.'

She glared at him, all the more irritated because he'd agreed with her so easily, so calmly, so less than effusive. Now she really felt like a good argument. She wanted to *win*, damn it.

His mouth twitched. 'So. You'll be organising the next one, then?'

She tossed her head back. Looked him straight in the eye. 'You're all challenge, aren't you, James?'

His eyes flared, flickered down. Then he drawled in that soft way that had all her senses on alert, 'So, my princess, are you.'

Instantly everything changed. The underlying cause of their intent awareness was pushed forefront. She forgot the party, forgot the job, could focus only on the here and now— on him and her and how they were going to sort each other out, finally. 'How are you going to handle this challenge, then?'

'You mean you?'

Her nod was slight, her body held still by the fiery, physical promise of his—so close but not quite there. She was sick of the way he held back.

'The way I always like to handle a challenge.' And suddenly he wasn't holding back. His fingers touched her shoulders again but it was different this time—firmer, more forceful. Sizzling. 'Hands on and in control.'

'Hands on is good.' She tilted her head back to look right into his face—to invite, to dare. 'But I don't believe you'll be in control.'

'Who'll be in control, then?' His head lowered, his gleaming eyes mesmerising her as he whispered the question.

'Neither of us,' she whispered back.

Amusement. Appreciation. Anticipation.

From his expression, he felt it too.

'I guess that way we'll be even.' His fingers traced over her collarbones. 'There's still one outstanding problem, though.'

'What's that?' She didn't want any more delays. She didn't want any more discussion.

Action was all she wanted now.

His smile widened and was as wicked as it could get. 'We still haven't worked out who's going to be on top.'

Her smile matched his in both intensity and naughtiness. 'The princess is always on top.'

'That right?' He was so close she could see the myriad golden brown flecks in his eyes and the way his pupils were swelling. 'We can start that way if you like, then see what happens.'

In the second she saw herself straddling his naked body, sanity stared her in the face. Sleeping with James would probably end in disaster. But her job was pretty much a disaster anyway. She might as well have the one experience she'd been wanting more than anything for the last three weeks. It would probably only be a one-off. She was, after all, just a party plaything. She already knew he didn't want anything more.

So why not be selfish, as everyone expected her to be, and do what *she* wanted? And she wanted him. Really badly, right now.

He knew. The confident strokes across her skin reflected his understanding. He wasn't asking. He didn't need to. He'd already started. His lips brushed her cheekbone and he muttered, 'It's time we dealt with it.'

Her eyelids fluttered at his caress. He kissed down her cheekbone and her eyes closed completely. She swayed forward, held her head up to his and parted her lips.

He kissed her then. And how he could kiss. Her glass slipped from her fingers and she collapsed into him, his arms tightened and she kissed him back, wanting to inflame him further. Wanting him to want her the way she did him—out of control, out of this world.

She thought of nothing, only let herself feel the sensations of his mouth on hers, his tongue searching, seeking the response she was only too happy to give.

His hands were blessedly firm on her body and she reached up, to run her hands down his back, measure his breadth and strength with the tips of her fingers, with the heel of her palm as she pressed him closer, circling her hips to press against his in the rhythm that came so naturally and that she knew would stir him into action.

He thrust one hand into her hair, holding the back of her head to his; the other hand pushed the small of her back, driving her belly into his hips, stopping her wriggles but making her more than aware of his hard erection. Without lifting his head he walked her backwards. She kept her eyes closed and let him, knowing he was getting them to his bedroom—to comfort and space. She was so hot she'd have taken him then and there—on the floor, the chair—she didn't care, she just wanted…

His hand lifted from her waist and she heard a click. Opening her eyes at last, she saw they'd made it to his room and he'd flicked on one of the bedside lights, giving a soft glow to the room. The thick curtains were drawn and the bed was big and some kind soul had already turned back the covering. The sheets were pale in the dim light and she looked forward to feeling their cool comfort on her burning skin...

She lifted her face for another kiss but he dropped to his knees, sliding his hands from her thighs to her feet.

She looked down as he circled his fingers and thumb around the bottom of each leg, amazed and enthralled at the sight of him, in a tux, on his knees at her feet. 'What are you doing?'

'Worshipping your ankles. You have the most shapely ankles and calves I've ever seen.'

'It's the high heels,' she explained, but feeling stupidly pleased by the compliment all the same.

'No. I've seen you walking barefoot in my office. Your legs are incredible.'

Sitting back on his heels, he toyed with her skirt, flaring out the material and creating a cool breeze on her thighs. She felt the need to rock against him again. Felt the need to make him move faster.

'Are you going to have a look under my dress?'

'I'm going to have more than a look.' His mouth was hot and open and wet as he began to press it on the start of her thigh, slowly moving across skin, and up. She stretched a hand down, reaching his hair, twisting her fingers through it, restlessly beginning to move against him. His jaw was warm and slightly rough and she wanted him to go even higher.

Suddenly he stood, with pleasure she saw the hint of breathlessness, the heightened colour in both his cheeks and eyes. Her hands lifted and she took the advantage, pressing her lower body to his and quickly unfastening the buttons on his shirt. She wanted to touch him, to taste him, to make him take her fast and furious. She kissed the expanse of golden skin, quick and hot kisses with her tongue flickering and her teeth nipping; she rocked faster against him, wanting to make him explode.

For moments he let her do it and she felt his tension building as he stood still under her ministrations. Then with a growl his hands came back to her hips, holding them while thrusting his forward to dig into her and she lifted her face to let his mouth plunder hers. She wanted to shriek yes as his kiss deepened, feeding and fuelling the hunger that had her so desperate.

He lifted his head away with a jerk, his breathing ragged, and he inhaled deeply through his nose. Damn. She knew he was going to make her slow down.

Grinning at her, he loosened his hard grip on her hips and slid fingers around her back, finding the zip secreted to the side. He tugged it down; she lowered her arms to let the straps fall.

Quickly, with a soft slither, the fabric slipped to the floor. His gaze followed the dress down. He was silent for a moment, his grin deepening. Then he stretched out a long, lone finger and ran it along the fine band of her black panties.

'Underwear.'

'Very thin, very sheer.' She held her tummy firm, trying to stop the shiver as his finger slid slowly from one side to the other.

'But still there.'

She nodded. 'Always.'

His grunt of laughter held a touch of mockery. 'Not so wild, princess?'

How little he knew. 'Too wild for you.' She pushed, taking him by surprise, and he stepped back, the bed butting behind his knees. She pushed again. He was ready that time but let her get away with it anyway, falling backwards and, with a bounce and a laugh, landed on his back.

'Well, then, climb on top, beautiful.'

Liss was used to being told she was beautiful, but he did more than just tell her. He made her believe it, simply by the look in his eyes—the almost painful passion in them.

She slipped her fingers beneath the thin panties and pulled them down with a shimmy and a wiggle. Stepping out of them, she twirled them on her finger before flinging them away. Propped up on his elbows, he watched her little stripper moment with humour that was underpinned by tense hunger.

She intended for him to become even more tense.

She got onto the bed on her knees and crawled her way up his body, keeping her torso lifted away from his. He could look but they weren't touching—not yet, not until she was positioned above the prize. Halfway up his body she settled on it. That magnificent, straining, hard ridge of him felt incredibly good through the slightly rough fabric of his trousers. When he was naked, it would feel even better, but right now it was fun just playing. Rubbing her hands over his golden, hair-sprinkled chest, she watched his want grow. This was what she wanted, to be straddling him, ready to take him. Her fingers worked the button on his trousers, wanting to feel him bare.

Instead of thrusting up to meet her as she expected, he suddenly scooted down the bed so it wasn't his pelvis beneath her but his chest. Their eyes met and his were dancing with desire and delight. She figured hers reflected a little shock.

He wriggled, sliding an arm under her leg, and with a twist got a shoulder under too and then he slid further beneath her. So it wasn't his chest she was astride, but his face.

Oh. My.

She froze, unable to decide what to do—move, not move.

His hands held her waist in place, taking the dilemma from her.

'James!' Heat scalded her as he turned his head and kissed the uppermost skin on her inner thigh, kissed again…and then…

She hadn't expected anything quite so intimate, quite so soon. Stupid perhaps, considering what they were doing, but this was…this was…

'What?' he asked lazily, fingers taking up where his tongue had left off. 'I thought you said you wanted to be on top.' His words were muffled and as he spoke the warm air against her sensitive skin sent delicious chills everywhere.

'I do, but this is…' She paused for breath as his tongue started another exploration. 'This is…' Her eyes closed as his mouth closed over her most sensitive point and he sucked. 'This is…just…really *good*.'

Incredibly intimate. Incredibly erotic.

Once more she twisted her fingers into his hair, literally hanging on to reality as he twisted fingers and tongue and lips into and around her.

Her whole body was hot and damp and breathing was difficult because even the air seemed fiery and it burnt her lungs. She screwed her eyes shut tighter as intense sensations closed in on her.

'James,' she muttered. Wanting the magic of release now, but wanting the moment to last for ever. Too good to last, too good to finish.

In answer he slid a hand up her stomach and beyond to find her breast, gently rubbing her nipple between forefinger and thumb. The burning breath shuddered out of her.

She stretched her arms forward, found the bed rails and

clung on with bone-crushing strength. She wanted to scream. She was going to scream. But she couldn't get it out for the difficult breaths and the half-sobs that she couldn't stop as he teased in a tormenting rhythm.

He slid both hands over her now, with firm strokes and then fluttering ones while he feasted on her. Tremors convulsed through her body and she repeated his name, almost broken.

'You still sure about being on top?' His sexy humour only served to heighten her almost painful pleasure.

She couldn't support herself any longer. The excitement was too intense and frankly all she wanted to do was lie back and enjoy it.

Toppling over to the side, she apologised. 'I'm sorry, James. When you do that I can't…'

'What, move?' He rolled, moving up the bed on all fours like a lion. She stretched out, happy to be his prey.

'Or think…' she murmured heavy-lidded as he paused at her breasts. 'Or speak…'

Indeed she could only moan then as he took her hardened nipple into his mouth and his fingers resumed their rhythmic rubbing.

He moved slowly over her—all the way down, then over again until every inch of her skin had been both burned and dampened with kisses and caresses. Until she lay without control over her own body, arching up in invitation, pleading with him—to have him inside and for the unbearable tension to be snapped by the ultimate sensation.

'James.' She shook her head wildly as he kissed the hollow at the base of her neck. It wasn't enough. It wasn't nearly enough. She had to have it all, now.

He left her body, left the bed, kicked off shoes, yanked down trousers and grabbed a condom from the complimentary pack in the drawer of the bedside table. All the while she lay supine, still arching her hips to his in time to that ancient rhythm, still whispering his name, because each time she did his eyes glowed and his hands shook.

His body was burnished with sweat. But still he could smile that slightly sarcastic smile and prove his point. 'If it's all right with you, princess, this time I'm on top.'

He was already back and settling his glorious weight on her when she abandoned all pretence and answered with ecstatic softness, 'Oh, yes.'

With a satisfied grin and a long, deliberate stroke he pushed hard inside. Her breath hissed out and she started shaking—the delight too pleasurable to bear.

He paused, the 'princess' he muttered half strangled. Then he moved.

She clung to his slick, broad shoulders, crying out as his body buffeted against hers again and again. He totally filled her—thrusting, making her take everything he had. And she fought to match him, curling her legs around his, pushing up to meet him, to drive him as much as he was driving her. Her gaze met and held by his. And the exquisite torture continued and sharpened, heightened and strengthened until she could no longer cope, could no longer control her ferocious response.

She arched high one final time and locked into a moment where she had never, ever felt so good. Her body clamped onto it—onto him, gripping him tight and hard until finally she convulsed, lost under waves of intense pleasure, hardly aware of her own scream.

CHAPTER TEN

SHE was awake but kept her eyes closed. Her highly accurate body clock told her it was still early. Very early. But she couldn't sleep a moment more. There was too much to stew over. Cataclysmic sex for one thing—she would never be the same.

So that was 'dealing with it', huh? She flexed her thigh muscles experimentally—just a touch. Yep, she definitely felt dealt with. James was incredible—as intense and in charge in the bedroom as he was in the boardroom. And already the runny-honey feeling inside was spreading, together with the lick of desire. She wanted to deal with him some too. So much for ensuring he was as much a slave to it as she was—she hadn't really got the chance last night.

She closed her eyes tighter. Last night. The party. Her screw-up. His challenge for another party.

Ugh.

When she finally opened her eyes she saw he was propped up on his elbow, studying her—alert, despite the unshaven look, the rumpled hair.

'Regrets?' he asked straight out.

'No.' Not sleeping with him. She could never regret that. Other elements? Maybe.

His mouth twisted into that cynical smile she didn't like so much. 'Of course. You're not the kind of person to have regrets.'

Did he still think she didn't feel things deeply? That she was completely shallow—just the party princess? She burrowed further under the sheet. Well, she wasn't going to admit to how deeply she'd felt a connection with him last night. How wonderful he'd made her feel.

'You think?' She tightened up. It wasn't from anticipation. 'Why, do you?'

'No. Not about that.'

OK. What, then? Something was clearly on his mind. But he wasn't about to share either. Not thoughts, not emotion. But maybe his body. The gold flecks had lit in his eyes.

'You know it was too good an experience not to be repeated,' he said softly.

Oh, she knew. She also knew he was ready for a repeat right now. And despite his blinkered vision of her, she couldn't refuse. Her body softened, her muscles ached to move. She quelled the delicious urge to stretch out every limb and curl her toes, savouring the tension as it knotted inside. And frankly she'd be more than happy to forget the party mess for a few more moments.

His fingers traced over her shoulders. 'You don't do serious.'

He wasn't asking. Apparently it was a given. Who said she didn't do serious? Admittedly up till now she hadn't. But things could change. Someone could make her feel differently about that. Lots of things felt unstable right now.

His gaze lifted from where he'd been watching his hand slide beneath the sheet along her breastbone, and he seemed to ensure he had her attention. 'I don't do serious either.'

'No.' But she didn't quite believe him. While he could flirt and be fun James was intense and focused and diligent and he'd do serious—with the right woman. It was just that she wasn't the right woman and he was making sure she knew that.

Fine. She wouldn't want serious with him anyway. He was too much the boss, too much in charge—mostly of himself. She itched to address that one.

'So, later today we work.' Both his gaze and hand dipped again. 'Right now, we play.'

What else was there to say? 'OK.'

He rolled onto her, claiming the dominant position, and she lay back and let him—for now, she reckoned. Just once more.

She'd always known James worked hard. Now she knew he played hard too. After another hour in bed—not sleeping— and half an hour in the shower—with barely time to soap— she was ready for a nap, but he was at the desk, hard at work.

Given what he'd asked her to do, she knew she had to knuckle under too. But she wondered if she was ever going to be able to keep up with him—in any arena. She wandered out of the bedroom to get set and discovered James had had her bags moved up from her room downstairs.

'We're going to be working night and day,' he said within earshot of the porter in the process of unloading the luggage trolley. 'It'll be easier for you just to crash in the other room.' His eyes were glinting and she was half amused and half maddened by the arrogance in his organisation of her. And she was alerted to the way he was protecting their reputations. He didn't want people talking either, huh?

'It's true,' he muttered, drawing her close after the porter had left. 'We don't have any time to waste.'

She didn't want to analyse what time they had, but did it anyway. Was it only the night? Only the week? Or only until he tired of her and sent her away?

She pulled away from him, quickly unpacked her clothes into the second bedroom, making the point that she still had her own space in the suite. Even if she did spend every sleeping moment in his bed, in his arms—and she badly wanted to—she also needed to keep some sense of independence. And she didn't want him breathing down her neck while she tried to get this party off the ground. Seeing he'd set up office in the main lounge, she moved her gear around the corner to the glassed-in balcony that gave spectacular views across the island.

She eased her stiff body into one of the large soft seats, powered up her laptop and pulled the portable phone nearer on the low table in front of her.

She could hear James already deep in conversation with some contractor or other on his mobile. How quickly he could switch from lust to business. She needed to learn that one too—pronto.

The first thing she had to do was organise the damn media. She wasn't going to be forgetting that one again. She typed up a list: glossy mags, newspapers, TV—she wanted all three. Plus photos on the hotel website. Podcast perhaps? He wanted coverage? He'd get coverage.

She'd get them in here early in the morning—or the night before if necessary. She'd ensure the hotel assigned them rooms all on the same floor—well away from any other guests. While the guests might court the media at the party, they needed their privacy too. Then the media could take a tour of the facilities during the day with the hotel manager and then be on hand for the party that night.

Rough plan in place, she started pulling together the

contact details for all of them. Over an hour later, list complete, it was time to start making the calls. Summoning courage, she dialled the first and gave him her spiel.

'But I heard there was a big bash there last night—extremely exclusive and no media present.'

She winced at the newshound's tone. She should have foreseen this kind of questioning. But she tried to gloss over it—inventing excuses wildly on the spot. 'There was a small function—the practice run, if you like. But this is the big one—the high-society event in the exclusive hotel that we're ready to show to the world.' *Practice run?* How ironic. And how on earth was she going to dig herself out of this?

'Little late for invites, isn't it?' Smart Alec journalist wasn't going to make it easy.

She knew he could smell a story, but she wasn't going to give him the tale of her humiliation. 'Things happen fast around here. If you're not interested...'

'We'll be there. Cameras can access all areas?'

'You won't be able to film the actual party, but certainly the set-up beforehand and the arrival of the guests. Still shots are fine inside the ballroom but obviously after a while we'd like you to be able to relax and enjoy the party.'

She was able to use her name to speak directly to the best photographers and journalists working for the best magazines. The magazines all wanted an exclusive but she refused to agree to it. They were all welcome—it was up to them to get the unique angle.

She repeated the conversation twenty times over. And was mighty glad there were only that many at that tier of media that she had to deal with directly.

Other paparazzi photographers would come anyway once news was out there was a media junket—local and foreign freelancers would camp out, hoping to get the 'shot' of the party that could be sold on to the exclusive magazines, even though they might have had their own photographers in place. It was all about that one shot.

It took hours—factoring in time differences and the fact it was the weekend. Then, as she got each to agree, she had to organise flights and email through the details for them. It took many hours.

With a sigh she sat back and stretched. She'd spent a whole day working on the party—promising something amazing—and hadn't even started planning it?

She choked back the nausea. And realised she'd only had orange juice all day. Never in her life had she sat so still and worked so hard for so long.

But it wasn't enough.

She tried to feel better about it. The bones were there. Good bones. The hotel was incredible. The chef would put something marvellous together. Aristo itself was beautiful…but these people were expecting something else again. And she had no idea how she was going to do it.

The anxiety was really starting to eat at her when James walked in with a hint of hungry and desperate in his face. All thought of the party fled because he caught her eye and grinned so wickedly and immediately her blood was on the move and anticipation quickened her lungs. He still wanted her. He wanted her right now.

She stood, legs no longer feeling stiff but supple and limbered instead.

He pulled his shirt off and beckoned. She followed. He didn't even need to *say* anything; she couldn't help but follow.

They'd barely got to the bedroom when he turned her into his arms and ran his hands down her sides and kissed her.

'So this is what you meant by "other duties as required",' she teased breathlessly minutes later, swirling her fingers into the light mat of hair on his chest.

'Hell, yeah.'

Later he phoned down to Reception, to where a skeleton staff were working, and requested they go to a restaurant and get a selection of whatever the finest dishes of the day were.

She slipped on a summer dress and he pulled on jeans and they ate in the conservatory overlooking the vibrant, affluent city.

Revived, she slanted him a saucy look, put her hand on his thigh, feeling his muscles move, liking the way he responded so quickly to so little.

They hadn't put the light on in their room so as night darkened the sky the city lights shone brightly—a very grown-up fairy-light display. They could see out but no one would be able to see them. Good thing, because by then they were naked and hot and dancing the most intimate of dances.

When she woke the next morning he'd already left the room. She stretched out a hand, could feel the lingering warmth on the sheet from his body. Could see the dent in the pillow pulled close to her own. She could really get used to this— the wild intimacy, the long cuddles… She froze. She'd better not get used to it—he'd already warned her it wasn't serious, it wasn't going to last. It probably wouldn't last more than this week—until she stuffed up this next event. Sheer panic filled her. How on earth was she going to pull off another party—even better than the other night? With almost no money and no time. She pushed the panic back and resolved to work through one issue at a time.

Guest list. As opposed to media list. She had to get invitations out as soon as possible. Fortunately she knew several of the out-of-town guests who had flown in specially were staying on for a week or so cruising round the island on board a luxury yacht. She had to get invitations to everyone today. But they'd be nothing like the handmade, pure silk, exclusive invitations of the first party.

She'd go very simple, very elegant and hopefully the guests would think it a little mysterious, not that she had no idea about a theme. She drew a mock-up on a piece of paper, then went to sweet-talk Stella, the hotel manager's secretary, who hopefully had more of an understanding of the desktop publishing program than she did.

Three hours later and the file was being emailed to the local printer to be printed. She spent another two hours in the office at the back of Reception figuring how to print the envelopes herself and then stuffing them. Then she sent the hotel porter to deliver them personally. In uniform, with a simple smart invitation—it wasn't brilliant but it wasn't bad. And right now it was the best she could do.

At that point she needed fresh air and a brain transplant— to have the smarts to pull the party out of a hat. She walked along the stretch of beach reserved exclusively for the hotel guests' use, looking up, down and all around for inspiration. She needed a theme but everything had been done to death— masked balls, black and white, tropical nights, pirates and princesses… Yeah, right. Yawn, yawn.

Décor was going to be a nightmare—especially given that James pretty much was prepared to pay only for the food and wine. While the hotel was beautiful, the ballroom all marble and light, how did she turn it into super-*super* special?

She'd gone with the simplicity of flowers last time—but not just any flowers. They'd been exotic, heady-scented orchids she'd had flown in specially and that had cost the earth.

She couldn't do that again. And what other options were
there? It wasn't as if she could get in a few helium cylinders
and just do balloons. It had to be more than that.

Where did you go from opulence? Aristo was the play-
ground of the rich and famous. Where they could come to
relax in privacy and also enjoy the high life should they
choose. And she'd given them a ball at which only the very
best had been on offer. It had been, she mused, one step away
from decadence.

She smiled. She'd jokingly accused James of wanting her
to arrange an orgy. She stopped still on the pristine sand.
Thought about that idea some more. What if she could gently
nudge the luxuriance of Saturday's ball on to an exclusive,
seductive evening, one that whispered the promise to fill the
appetite for pleasure—all kinds of pleasure?

She racked her brains, trying to remember more than
mere fragments of the Classical Studies she'd taken at uni-
versity. The ancient Greeks knew how to throw parties—
orgies by another name. What if she created a setting in
which that spirit could be invoked? Decadent, hedonistic—
as James had accused her of being—could she turn that to
her advantage? Create a sumptuous, sensual feast but one
that could somehow still be refined and elegant? Was that
even possible?

Yes. She could make it work. It was the only real idea she'd
had and, besides, it tickled her naughty bone. Right now
James made her feel like a sensual goddess. It wouldn't last,
of course. But maybe she could tempt him with fruits and
wines and keep him under her spell for just that little longer.

Her blood tingled with excitement. The other night she'd
imported everything. This time she couldn't do that—she would
look at traditional produce and plenty of it. She retraced her

steps back to the hotel, fast and on fire, ideas sparking one after the other, finally feeling as if she'd had a breakthrough—maybe she could put it all together after all. She was back in charge.

CHAPTER ELEVEN

JAMES sat at his desk and tried not to dwell on the fact Liss had been gone for hours, that he was missing her, and that he wanted her again badly. One night hadn't been enough. Nor had two. Not nearly enough. Her body had him bound, and now he found he wanted to know more—wanted to get inside her head as much as he had her pants. He wanted to understand what it was that made her frown in her sleep, what it was that caused her to look wistful when she thought she was alone. He'd seen it in Sydney, he'd seen it here. He wanted to know why and he also, simply, still *wanted* her.

He looked up as the door opened and immediately gave thanks to whoever was the god of lust. She floated in wearing a sophisticated dress as casually as if it were old jeans and tee. Only she could wear clothes like that with such seemingly effortless panache. He couldn't help the way his whole body tightened.

She leaned back against the door to close it. Then he noticed her expression. And his body tightened even more.

He'd seen that gleam once before—when she'd nearly-but-not-quite kissed him. He knew what it meant—that he was in trouble. And, oh, boy, he wanted to be. She turned and he heard the lock slide home. Then he heard a zip slide.

He barely noticed his pen slip from his fingers. Too busy noticing the way she moved. A tall glowing goddess had entered the room and seemed to promise to fulfil his every fantasy.

'It's afternoon tea time, James.'

'Is it?' Did the words make it from thought to audible?

The seductress stepped closer. 'Fancy some?'

He cleared his throat and tried for casual. 'Why not?'

Her amused glance told him she knew he was all knotted up. Somehow, she whisked the dress, despite its intricate straps, straight up over her head and off. Her bra and panties were pretty and pale and pink but with simple, sultry movements she had them off too and he had to admit he liked what was under them even more.

Her lithe, slim body was now completely nude except for wisps of shoes. He looked slowly back up from the floor— her long shapely legs, the cute neat arrow of hair between her legs, the narrow waist, the jut of her breasts and their large, hardened nipples, her long neck and long silky hair. But what turned him on most was the desire in her face, the melt in her dark chocolate eyes, the deliciously sinful smile. She was out for some fun. And he was only too happy to oblige.

She turned her back to him and bent over a small table, giving him the sublimely sexy view of her beautiful bare rounded bottom and the inviting crevasse between.

He was held fast by warring desires. Part of him ached to bury his face in her. To tickle, tease and taste her with his tongue until her hips writhed, her hands pulled at his hair and she screamed out his name.

The other part wanted to simply hold her close so he could push himself inside and pump hard and fast, over and over until she clamped tight around him, her hands clinging to his shoulders, and, yes, she screamed out his name.

Maybe he'd do both.

But right now he couldn't move. She had that look in her eye and he had to sit back and wait to see exactly what she was going to do.

She stood up, gave him a saucy glance and he saw she'd retrieved a condom from the small drawer in the table. Have mercy.

The gentle sway of her hips as she walked towards him was riveting. She tore open the small packet as she moved. His trousers were painfully tight. He'd never felt the blood pump as much as it was now. Never felt so hard it was this painful.

'What about foreplay?'

She put the condom on the desk. 'That was it.'

He tried to breathe again but he found he couldn't manage even that. Too hot. Too hard.

She pushed out his chair a little and spun it around to face her. She looked down and saw the bursting tent of his trousers. 'In a little trouble, James?'

Her fingers stroked down his rigid body. It wasn't soothing.

'Just a little,' he rasped.

She smothered a giggle as she undid the top button and then tried to slide the zip down. 'Not little, James. More like colossal.'

He muttered a swear word or ten and grasped the material each side of the button and hole in each hand and pulled them apart hard—the sound of the material ripping was incredibly satisfying. His cotton boxers were in the way too so he just ripped them as well.

Her eyes were wide and her pupils swollen and her smile just kept growing too. So did he.

He shifted his hips restlessly.

'Sit still,' she ordered.

Surprised, he looked up at her. Met the challenge in her eyes and felt his body winch even tighter, even harder.

She stepped close, reached out and began unbuttoning his shirt. As she leant forward to spread the halves back he pressed his mouth to her collarbone. Her smile was sublime as she stood back.

He gripped the arms of the chair as she rolled the condom down on him with those tormenting slow fingers.

Finally she knelt, jamming one knee either side of his hips in the narrow chair. Rising above him, she spread her legs to take him. And all he could do was watch and wait and feel— more turned on than he'd ever been. Again. By her.

She closed her eyes as she took just the tip of him in. He let out the gust of air he'd been holding on to. She was tight and he was big and he felt her stretch to take him inch by slow, incredible inch.

Her eyes flashed open and stared straight into his. 'You feel good.'

Understatement. He felt fantastic.

And she slipped slowly up and down, rotating her hips around him, a sensuous, slow dance than was officially sending him crazy.

The fantastic feeling increased but demand rose hard too and soon the urge to drive deep into her gripped him. He had to master, to conquer, to take her body and make it shake and shudder in surrender. Instinct told him to have her as bound by lust as he now was. Every muscle burned with the need to move more—harder, faster, deeper. And yet she held still, in charge above him.

He thought of phone numbers, stock prices, hotel listings…anything to stop him, to slow himself down. He even resorted to chanting the alphabet song—but he only got as far as F and he knew he was in trouble. He tried to start again.

Finally, with profound relief, he saw her control begin to waver. Her breathing was raw and he could see the torture in her eyes as she neared climax. The want in her expression increased and he shifted his hips just that little bit, wanting her to know the power was there.

Liss rose up and almost off him, watching the frustration in his face sharpen. She could just about see him reciting sums in his head. She knew he wanted faster, harder—so did she. But she loved the look on his face as she teased him. Loved leaning forward and teasing his lips with the tips of her nipples. He was groaning in a way she'd never heard him groan, only barely hanging on. His eyes were glazed, his skin damp, and she felt all his muscles bunch even tighter. His face was a twisted picture of pleasure and pain as his control was pushed to the absolute limit. She wanted him broken.

'I need to…' He couldn't seem to get the rest out. 'I need to…'

'What, James?' she murmured into his ear as she slid down on him again, taking him in to the hilt. She saw his lips moving but couldn't make out the words.

She whispered once more. 'What are you saying?'

'The alphabet… I'm singing the alphabet.'

'Are you crazy?' She tried to laugh but it came out more of a sob. She took his face in her hands, determined to set him free. 'Look at me. *Feel* me.' She rode him that bit harder. 'Come in me.'

'What about you?' Teeth gritted, the effort of holding back biting even sharper into his features.

She smoothed the strain from his damp forehead. 'I'm already one step ahead of you.'

He stopped the light caresses over her back. Came to grip her hips. And with incredible strength he took her weight with his hands, the muscles in his arms bunching. Holding her a fraction above him so he could lean back in the chair and pump upwards. Hard. Fast. Frantic.

The base of his pelvis ground against hers, closer and closer. And suddenly she was the one groaning and he was the one with the diabolical grin. His fingers hurt but she didn't care, barely noticed in fact—too close to experiencing ecstasy.

It was only another stroke and then it hit. Another freedom-destroying orgasm in which she cried out, caught between tears and laughter, and then she revelled in his loud shout and the violent spasms of his strong body as he finally lost all control.

'You're a witch,' he muttered, chest heaving as he still struggled for breath five minutes later.

She smiled, spread all over him as soft as melting creamy butter and totally pleased with herself. 'I really like being on top.'

Without doubt he understood her enjoyment of the situation—her success. His eyes narrowed. He lifted her up, set her on her feet again, and then stood up. He took her hand and started walking—fast. Legs wobbly, she struggled to keep up with him as in only a few paces he crossed the room and went into the bedroom. She almost stumbled, such was his speed. He turned, scooped her up and with a devilish smirk literally tossed her onto the bed.

Hungry excitement, which she had thought just filled, stirred again in her belly.

'What are you doing?' She knelt up as he shrugged off his shirt and stepped out of the remnants of his trousers and undies.

He pushed her back onto the bed again and leant over her, teeth showing in a wide, wicked grin. 'Showing you exactly who's boss.'

Later that night she sat at the computer, Googled the ancient Greek rituals surrounding the 'orgiastic festivities' of Dionysus, and giggled. She was definitely going to go stylised, just a hint or two, not full on and out there. But from where was she going to get the hint, the flavour of naughty fun? The computer search threw up a lot of images—artists' impressions of those decadent scenes. They'd be perfect—but as if the Louvre or the British National Gallery were going to loan priceless paintings for a party? Maybe she could project some of the more famous images onto the walls of the ballroom? She frowned—it was a possibility but not perfect. And she wanted perfect.

And that was when she remembered Camille—the friend with whom she'd studied Art History whilst in Paris. Whose parents lived in what anyone else would call a gallery—such was their art collection. And she remembered the tapestries Camille's mother had—the ones Camille's father relegated to a different wing, declaring they weren't really 'art'. It was a loving argument between them—art versus craft, oil on canvas versus textiles and yarn. Maybe she'd have some Greek scenes in there? All Liss remembered was that there were hundreds of them, many locked away in cupboards and not even out on display. She refined her Google search.

After finding what she wanted, she checked on James— he'd fallen asleep on the sofa, feet on the table in front of him. She'd quickly learned that when James slept, he really slept— with the same kind of dedication and wholeheartedness that he approached everything in life. So, knowing he couldn't hear, she picked up the phone and called.

'I'm in a bit of a fix,' she explained once the necessary squeals and brief catch-ups were concluded. She gave a quick overview of the party—skipping over the fact it was totally last minute to make up for the one she'd botched. 'Can I borrow some of those tapestries your mum has?' She detailed exactly which ones.

'Those old things? For a *party*?'

Admittedly they were old, but the way Camille described them was hardly flattering. Liss grinned. With the right lighting, music, food and atmosphere those 'old things' would help transform the palatial ballroom into the intimate space she wanted. The thickly woven material with its gold thread and full-bodied colours would heighten the sense of richness and luxury—the intricacy and skill in each would reflect the master craftsmanship in the construction of the hotel itself. And they were just that little bit different.

'If you can get them there, you can use them.'

Brilliant.

Damn.

The thoughts struck simultaneously. How was she going to manage to get them here? No way could she put the cost of transport from Paris on the account. All the extras—the décor, the finishing touches—were having to be done on the cheap. The cost of airlifting several huge tapestries from Paris to Aristo wouldn't come anywhere near cheap. But she had her heart set on them. Knew they'd make the night, set the scene, and the rest would happen naturally.

'Will you come to the party too?' she asked Camille. It would be so great to have a friendly face there.

'Can't, darling. I'm off to New York.'

They talked some more—caught up on commonalities, on gossip.

'Thank you so much.' Liss wrapped up the call some twenty minutes later. 'I'll organise transport for them and be back in touch.'

Transport. She drummed her fingers on the table. If only she could access some of her trust fund. It would be nothing to her. But that had been blocked and she only had her day-to-day account and her earnings from her few weeks working for James. She looked up her account online. She had some money. But she'd mentally ring-fenced it for a new dress. Stupidly she hadn't brought another party outfit with her and she had nothing new to wear to this do. She gritted her teeth. On the dress she was going to have to improvise. She'd use the money she had to get the tapestries sent over. Besides she could always wear the frock she'd worn last week.

Ugh. She shuddered. It went against every fashion rule.

She wanted the party to be different, wanted to be wearing something new and different herself. But, as she remembered James's words with a little wince, it wasn't all about *her*.

She walked across the lounge, looked at where he lay sprawled—undoubtedly uncomfortably—on the sofa. The sight made her smile. It was the second night in a row she'd stayed in—she couldn't remember the last time that had happened. But how nice it was, just the two of them in their apartment in the sky—like a little nest. She had no desire to leave it, no desire to get dressed up and go dancing. She'd join him on the sofa except he was hogging it. She bent and studied him. He was sleeping the well-earned sleep of the hardworking achiever. But he badly needed to get to a bed or he'd have a crick in his neck and probably a bad case of the grumps with it.

She had no way of getting him there without disturbing

him. She went tingly all over with anticipation. Oh, well. Disturb him she must.

But she did it gently, raining soft kisses all over his face, running her fingertips over his rough jaw and down his throat. She felt the ripple in the muscles beneath her as Mr Deep Sleeper slowly became aware.

Eventually his eyes opened, dark with desire. 'I was dreaming about you,' he muttered, his voice husky, a little rusty. 'And here you are.'

'Here I am,' she agreed, pressing another kiss to his sleep-warm skin. The scent of sensuality in the air sharpened. He moved, lifting his arm across her back to hold her to him. She could feel the strength she had awakened. No escaping now.

'Are you going to make the rest of my dream come true?' he murmured.

Be his fantasy playmate? He was hers already—nothing could have prepared her for the way he fulfilled her every sensual wish. 'I will if you tell me what to do.'

For a moment their gaze met and held, and the passion flamed between them. Then, with his eyes, he told her. With his hands. With his words. And she had no hesitation complying and going, as always, that one step further, rejoicing when he shook and shouted—out of control, utterly in lust. Exactly as she wanted him—with none of the bruising mask of sarcasm, just naked need. And she knew from his response that their physical journey together was far from over. The relief was immense.

Liss worked alone in the conservatory at the laptop. James spent most hours of the day either in meetings or locked in telephone and video conference calls. This time she wished he'd take more of an interest in what she was doing. She badly wanted to ask him what he thought, whether what she had come up with so far was going to be OK. She didn't have any of the over-confidence she'd had only last week. Things seemed to be slipping from her.

But he was so obscenely busy she knew the last thing he needed was tedious neediness from her. She was distracting him enough in other ways as it was. She was the first thing he reached for when walking back in after a few hours' absence and at night they had quite some time active in bed before actually getting to sleep.

He seemed to have no interest in being her boss any more—it was lovers' talk, lovers' laughter. She was the good time, the light relief, the relaxation in his spare moments. That was the role assigned to her—the box for her to be kept in.

And so, when he appeared in the doorway, she pulled on her perky persona. It was what he expected, after all. And she was determined to hide from him how wobbly she was feeling—not just about the party but about everything, especially him.

He'd awakened in her feelings she'd never experienced— a longing to be with him long term. She'd never thought of permanence before; now it was all she thought of. She pushed the fantasy from her mind and forced herself to focus, knowing it could only be a temporary fling. He'd told her so. His lust would be filled and he'd send her away.

She was always being sent away.

But even though she knew that, it didn't stop her from trying to fight the inevitability of it—working harder, wanting to do such a wonderful job that he'd want her to stay.

She needed to work out something exceptional with the lighting—forget the impending heartache and focus on achieving something amazing. At first she'd thought candles, little votives or tea lights everywhere—creating a lover's grotto. The flicker of warm light would flatter the skin of the beautiful people in attendance. Except, it would be a major fire and safety risk, the little candles would have to be replenished halfway through the evening—a complete hassle—and there was no way she could have the tapestries hanging in a smoke-filled atmosphere. So, the lighting was going to have to be electric. While the chandelier was magnificent, she wanted something more. Fairy lights could work. But like every other idea it had been done to death. And they'd look tack-a-rama next to the majestic chandelier.

What she needed was some good advice. Not James—too busy of course. And she needed to do this herself, wanted to surprise him, wanted to give him the intimate he'd joked about that night at the art gallery.

She could only turn to the familiar. The club she used to frequent as a teenager had always had an awesome light show and special effects and she went to see Ben, the owner, late in the afternoon. It didn't go so well.

'You want me to do this basically for free?'

'Everyone will know who provided the lighting—it'll be in the media kit—huge publicity for you.'

'You had a ball there last week, didn't you? Weren't any of those contracts paid either?'

Awkwardly Liss shuffled her feet. 'This situation is a little different. I need a favour here, Ben. For old times' sake?'

'Shame you didn't think to ask me last week. I heard half the contractors were flown in from as far away as Australia.'

Liss wanted to kick herself for her stupidity. She'd got half the locals offside for flying in her own team—killing the budget and destroying what goodwill she might have had. A few summers partying at Ben's club several years ago obviously wasn't enough.

'It's a top night at the club—we need the gear here,' he said gruffly. 'I can't help you, princess.'

Liss stared at him amazed—aghast. 'But, Ben—'

He turned away. Literally turned his back on her. She was left standing, feeling foolish. In the end she had no option but to walk out—alone and empty-handed.

She tried another club only to discover her old 'friend' was now barely an acquaintance, uninterested and unable to assist. She left that one more quickly than the first, decided to try just one more. The streets seemed dark and foreign. She couldn't believe it—this was her home turf and yet she felt like an unwelcome stranger.

She started to wonder if there was anyone on Aristo who she could turn to. None of the people she'd thought she could count on were willing to help her out. Had she been away so long they'd forgotten? Or hadn't they been her friends in the first place? Had they only encouraged her company back then because she brought in more customers? Now she no longer lived here she didn't have that to offer—and they weren't interested. Humiliation seeped into her. She felt like such an idiot. Such a naïve fool to have thought they might actually have liked her for her. It was all about the publicity, the crown, the money. She stood outside the third club and had to dig deeper for the courage to go in. She didn't stay long—could tell from the manager's face that he wasn't willing. She didn't want to try any more—just wanted to slink back to the hotel, lick her wounds and build her defences. But James was there and with James she needed more defences than ever. Rejection threatened her from all sides.

* * *

The next day James surprised her as she sat staring at her laptop, despairing.

'Come and have lunch with me.'

They took a taxi into the heart of Ellos, selected a small restaurant that had privacy and fast, excellent food. They sat and she looked through the menu. He got a message on his Blackberry and, with an apology by way of a wink, sat and tapped out a reply.

Knowing how long he might take and how hungry she was, she summoned the waiter and ordered for both of them.

He looked up as the waiter departed, surprise on his face.

'Is what I ordered for you OK?' She smiled.

'It's exactly what I would have ordered.' He switched off the Blackberry and pushed it to the side.

She'd observed him at enough dinners and seen him hoovering enough hors d'oeuvres to understand his appetite. 'I know what you like.'

He regarded her, the glint in his eye steady but somehow more intense. 'That you do.'

Her tingling sensation spread from the inside out. It wasn't just desire that he was reflecting. He seemed to be looking at her with fresh eyes—could see more clearly—and he liked what he saw even more. A little thrown, she put the focus back on him.

'Do you always work this hard?' He rarely seemed to have time out. But he never complained. He seemed to thrive on it.

'My father ground a strong work ethic into us. It didn't matter that we were born into wealth. We were still expected to prove ourselves—to succeed independently.'

And he had of course. And she knew he thought the same couldn't be said of her. 'What would happen if you didn't?'

He blinked. 'There's no question we wouldn't. You put in the work, you get there.'

'You really think it's that simple?'

They both sat back as the waiter placed their plates. 'Sure. With effort everyone gets there eventually.'

Ha. She knew all about putting in effort and still not quite making it. But then, maybe her effort hadn't quite been big enough. 'How many brothers and sisters do you have?'

'Two brothers.'

'Let me guess, you're the eldest.'

His smile was immediate. 'How did you figure that?'

'You're responsible. Perfectionist. You've taken on the family expectations and more than met them. And if you're going to get into trouble you've learnt to do it discreetly.'

He chuckled. 'So what about you?'

'I'm just one of the spares.' She shrugged, losing her appetite for her Caesar salad.

'And fast learned getting into trouble publicly gives you the attention you need?'

Why would being yelled at and then sent away be what she needed or wanted? But she hid the pain, shrugged off his gentle ribbing with a playful smile. 'Maybe.'

He spent a moment concentrating on his freshly steamed fish, then asked, 'If you weren't a princess what would you do? What would you want to be?'

She sensed a trap. And she decided not to answer in the way he wanted—things were the way they were. 'There's no point thinking that way. It's what I am. The princess thing is literally bred into me. It's the way I was born—like the colour of my eyes and hair.'

'You can change the colour of your hair. And the style.'

'Why would I want to?' She put her fork down and pushed

the plate away. 'Why are you so determined to change me? I am what I am, James. This is it.'

'Is it? It feels to me like there's more to you than the party image you project.'

'Don't go looking for things that aren't there.' She needed to listen to her own advice. Not go looking for friendliness or tenderness or understanding—the elements she was all too tempted to read in his expression.

'You make out like you're so surface, so selfish, and yet you give of yourself in ways that I don't think even you're aware of.'

Her laughter was brittle. 'Give what, James? I shop, I party. That's it.'

'You also like helping people. You like putting them at their ease. You're generous with your time and spirit.' He paused. 'You're generous with me.'

Of course she was. She liked him—but right now she wished he'd let her be at ease. She didn't want to peel back whatever other layers were there. Soon, probably very soon, he would send her away. She already knew that—even if he hadn't made it clear that this wasn't anything more than a playful fling, she knew to expect it because it was what always happened. She wasn't wanted—not long term, not by anyone. Not her family. Not her lover.

And if she revealed everything to him, his rejection would hurt all the more. And she didn't need the humiliation of the pity and embarrassment he'd feel if he found out what he was starting to mean to her. It was best to keep up the front so he wouldn't discover how much more she wanted—to love and be loved.

But still he probed. Leaning in, asking the question with an air of invitation, of intimacy. 'What's the one thing in the world you don't have but that you want?'

For an infinitesimal moment she closed her eyes, seeing it

immediately. A house she could call her own. A collection of cafés and cute boutiques on the corner of the street. A sense of permanence. A place to belong. And no threat of ejection or rejection.

A home—something she never seemed to have had.

He'd laugh, of course. And if she bared her secret dreams to him, she bared her hurts as well. She didn't need those sharpened and highlighted by his sarcastic wit. So quickly she came up with an answer appropriate for a superficial party princess. 'An unlimited supply of designer dresses and shoes—for free.'

He leant even closer, eyes laser-sharp. 'That wasn't the first thing that came into your mind.'

'What makes you say that?'

'Because for a moment your face went all soft and wistful. Then you thought up the answer you gave me and you closed over again.'

She flinched. Abandoned the idea of eating altogether. Damn him for being so observant.

'What was that first thought?'

'You're so clever, you work it out.'

He sat back and regarded her with that look of mocking challenge. She hoped he didn't mean it too seriously. 'Maybe I will.'

CHAPTER TWELVE

SOME things were falling into place. Others weren't. And Liss's brain was becoming too scrambled to work properly. In the last few days she'd had the wildest, sweatiest sex she'd ever experienced. James hadn't been kidding—he never stopped until she screamed. Time and time again he made her orgasm until her whole body ached and she was begging for a break. But inside she was begging for more: more physical and for more than just physical. The stress of both the party-planning nightmare and coping with his potent sensuality was exhausting her.

James was becoming her total focus. She *really* liked him. He didn't have to give her this chance. Anyone else would have sacked her weeks ago. And she knew it wasn't just because they were sleeping together that he was giving her another opportunity to redeem herself. He wanted to believe the best in people. He wanted people to be the best they could be. He expected it of himself and he expected it from everyone else too. But he was fair enough to understand that people might need more than one shot at it. That not everyone was as capable as he.

But she also knew he was no pushover. There wouldn't be

chance after chance. This was it. More than anything she didn't want to disappoint him. Ultimately, she knew she would. She always did.

Still she was determined to try and make the party the best it could be. So when she was gone he'd look back on this time and not see her as a complete failure, a complete flake. She didn't want him to send her away but it was inevitable—she'd do something stupid—or not do something sensible—and it would all be over. Or he'd simply fall out of lust with her.

She tried to forget him—for a few minutes at least while she fixed the party. Entertainment was now the biggest problem. She wanted something sophisticated in the early part and then the funkiest DJ to kick up the dance floor later in the evening. But none of her old contacts were interested so she'd have to try some of the newer clubs in town. And she'd have to go and listen to them to see if they would be OK. She could sneak out and listen to part of the set and be back in an hour or so. No way would James want to go with her—he was so busy and she could see the strain of tiredness in his eyes. She wouldn't bother him with it. After all, it was her mess to sort out.

In the middle of the night, as the club scene was starting to swing, she crept out. She hated leaving the warm cocoon that was his bed. He was sleeping soundly, relaxed, so attractive. For once she didn't want to be in a crowded atmosphere, the music blaring. As it was the DJ was dreadful and she was ready to cry with frustration.

When she got back into bed, almost two hours later, he stirred, rolling towards her, half waking as he felt her hands.

'You need warming up,' he muttered.

She did because inside all she felt was the coldness of failure and the disappointment of being let down by people she'd thought she could count on.

* * *

The next day she trawled the streets, finally finding some success for the lighting at the local amateur-dramatic society. There was a kid there, who looked about sixteen, who'd done a 'marvellous job' for the local panto show. All Liss could hope was that he wouldn't wire the place funny and burn it down in some freak accident.

She spent hours talking through the plans with the head chef and maître d'.

'Last week it was all the best the world has to offer. This time, with the media on us, let's showcase Aristo—the best *we* have to offer. But we're on a tight budget.' She grinned. 'It's a real test for you.'

'I'll say.' The chef still looked anxious, despite having had a few days to get used to the idea.

'You get what I'm after, right?'

'Sure.'

Walking back through she noticed the unusual asymmetrical skirt Stella, the hotel secretary, was wearing. 'Where did you get your skirt?'

Stella looked pleased. 'My boyfriend made it. He's a designer.'

Liss looked a little closer at the outfit—checking the clean cut, the tight stitching, the young and funky style. Interesting. 'Does he have a shop?'

'Oh, no, nothing like that. He's only just finished at design school.'

'You mind if I get his number?'

Looking surprised, Stella gave it to her and Liss arranged to see him right then.

'Princess Liss.' Tino, Stella's man, greeted her casually, as if it were every day that a member of royalty visited his 'coolly ramshackle' apartment. She looked at his sketches and the pieces he'd made for his final portfolio and made up her mind immediately.

'You want me to what?' he asked a few minutes later.

'The most glamorous party dress you can come up with.'

'In two days?' He didn't sound staggered, but he did seem a little sceptical—of her. 'You don't usually wear unknown designers.'

True. It was always exclusive and unbelievably expensive. She smiled. 'After this, you won't be unknown any more.'

He looked her over critically. 'You're even thinner in real life than you are in the photos.'

She knew she'd lost a little weight this week. It didn't take much for it to be noticeable. 'Will you be able to do it?'

'You know I can't say no.'

'Thank you.'

'You have to let me do my thing though—no interference.' He came across very sure of himself—but, judging from his work, Liss thought maybe he had the right to be.

She took a deep breath. 'So long as I look decent, you have free rein.'

'Great.' He suddenly looked like a kid in a candy shop and she hoped like hell she could trust her instincts.

'There's something else.' She was glad she'd remembered. 'I need an army of waiters and waitresses who look really good.'

'The local modelling agency,' Tino replied promptly. 'If the world's media are going to be there, they'll do it all for free.'

Of course they would. Young starlets, hungry for fame, would leap at the chance to be snapped at the ultimate society ball. 'Not free, but standard service rates, OK?'

'Sure. I can organise it if you like. What do you want them to wear?'

'I haven't the budget for outfits to be custom made. Nor

do we have the time. But somehow they have to look fabulous, uniform—it needs to be obvious they're there to help but in keeping with the theme.'

'Classical, right?'

'Classical with a hint of naughty.'

'Kind of like you, princess.'

She managed a sort of smile.

He looked thoughtful. 'Every model worth her weight in diamonds has a Calvin Klein tee shirt.'

She looked sideways at him. 'Tee shirt? We're talking the ultimate in glamour, Tino.' What had she got herself into? What on earth was he going to have her wearing?

He flicked his fingers. 'Don't worry, leave it to me.'

With the amount of things she had to do, and the amount of time in which to do them all, she didn't have much choice.

Friday afternoon she finally got to see her old friend Cassie. It wasn't for long and as she walked back to the hotel she hoped that James wouldn't be there. She needed a little time because right now she was feeling wobblier than a three-quarters-set jelly. Seeing Cassie had been more upsetting than she'd expected and if James was in one of his intrusive, cynical moods she'd lose it.

But he was there, stuck at the desk, up to his neck in paperwork, shirt sleeves rolled up. She gave him a bit of a smile and moved to the little balcony. Opened up the laptop and stared at the budget she'd put together for the party. The columns and rows blurred together. Eyes that had been dry for so long filled and the tears that threatened burnt them, making them water all the more.

James stepped round the corner. 'Are you OK?'

'Fine,' she replied briefly, still staring at the screen. 'Just a bit tired.'

'Did you catch up with your friend?'

She nodded, blinking. 'It was great.'

She felt mortified that she'd sent Cassie fluffy letters and silly postcards—where the biggest concern she'd related had been which party to go to at the start of Fashion Week. She'd had no idea of the struggle and trauma Cassie had been through—the secrets she had been keeping. Liss's own hurts were laughable compared to that and she had no right to be feeling this tiny spurt of envy.

She'd felt it as Cassie had bent to listen to the small boy when he'd burst into the room for a minute before dashing back out again. Cassie's face had illuminated, the love plain for anyone to see. It had tugged at Liss in a spot she didn't know she had until that moment.

Cassie had told Liss some more of what had happened all those years ago. Not that much, but Liss could read between the lines and had seen the shadow of vulnerability flash in her face. And now Cassie was so happy. Liss felt such a tide of thankfulness wash over her—that her friend had found the love and joy she deserved. Sebastian had abdicated—given up an entire kingdom for her.

Liss couldn't imagine anyone offering her that kind of whole, unwavering, unconditional love. She didn't deserve it. She'd been nothing but frivolous—modelling, partying, offering no real depth or contribution. So she did some charity work—a little, but not a lot—and what of it? Not as much as she could or should given her position.

And where did she go from here? Now Alex was Prince Regent and looking for the diamond, the instability meant there was no way he'd let her come back for fear she'd set off even more wild headlines. But in truth she'd been isolated from her country for so long it didn't even feel like home any more. The places she'd gone to as a teen had turned their backs on her—going out these last couple of nights had been no fun, alone and unsupported.

James had been right back in Sydney. She was lost. And she didn't know where or how she was going to find what she wanted.

'She must have been pleased to see you.' He was still standing in the doorway, watching her.

Their lives were poles apart. Cassie had laughed and hugged Liss when she'd apologised for how trite her letters must have seemed, told her not to be silly, that they'd lit her up for days.

But they had had different priorities—Cassie had real ones: to care for her child, and now to love and be loved by her husband. Liss ached for that sort of fulfilment. Instead here she was still making the same mistakes she'd been making five years ago—looking for love, for acceptance in all the wrong places. What a fool she'd been for so long. Now, when she wanted things to be different, she didn't know where to start.

'Yeah.' She looked harder at her screen. The party—she'd focus on the party. But she saw the blank spot under 'entertainment'. She was so desperate she was seriously considering doing a compilation on her MP3 player and feeding it into the ballroom's sound system. She blinked again—hoping that by magic something would appear under the heading. And she wished James would go back to his desk so she could get over the moment of self-pity. She could see him out of the corner of her eye, studying her, making her feel self-conscious.

The next thing she knew he stepped forward and pushed the lid of her laptop down. She looked up in horror.

'It saves automatically.' He smiled away her anxiety. Then she saw the warmth in his expression. She hurriedly looked down at the computer again. When he looked like that he seemed so dangerously approachable. She couldn't afford to unload to him. Probably by the time they went back to Sydney their affair would be over. It was only until the attraction went away, after all. Was it for him already? For her it was only worsening. She couldn't admit that to him, couldn't admit to any of the turmoil inside. She'd sound like some silly, needy girl. She had everything—youth, looks, fame and fortune. How could she complain? Spoilt wasn't the word.

All she wanted was to lie in bed and be held and, damn it, maybe even cry. But she didn't want to admit she was tired—didn't want him to think she couldn't handle either hard work or him.

He seemed to understand anyway—part of the problem at least. 'I'm tired too.' He took her hand and tugged her up. 'Come on. We need a rest.'

She didn't think a rest was what he had in mind and she didn't know if she was up to anything much more. But he surprised her. He pushed her onto the bed, set about removing her clothes, not with passionate ardour but with caring gentleness that made her heart ache all the more. After stripping himself, he slipped under the covers with her and just cuddled up behind her, his arms warm and strong as they surrounded her.

She turned to look at him, saw the gleam under his heavy lids. The passion was there but he was reining it in. And then it seemed she did have a little energy. She couldn't lie here and not touch him. And she was filled with an almost desperate need to have him want her despite his obvious exhaustion. She had to know that the need for each other was greater than the need for anything else—that he wasn't tired of her already, that it wasn't almost over.

She kissed him, set the spark to the smoulder, and as she kissed him her desperate need opened up. She was lost. She didn't have the energy to keep up her front any more and with her mouth, with her arms, she took and she took and she took. This was raw. This was real. The depth of feeling was totally foreign to her. And she couldn't hide how much it affected her. She twisted in his arms, unable to get enough of his caresses, unable to satisfy her need to touch him.

'Enjoying yourself, princess?' he asked as she pulled at his shoulders, encouraging him to move over her.

'Oh, James…' she breathed as he pushed inside her slick, wet space. She lifted her hips to ease his entry, letting him slide all the way in one smooth stroke.

God, she loved this. She loved him. She muttered his name again, tears building beneath her closed lids as the enormity of the moment, the realisation of her emotion, hit her.

'Oh, James, what?' he asked.

She heard it then, the familiar touch of sarcasm. The slight mockery rasping underneath the note of desire. He retained sense while she was spinning so dizzily under a tide of love. Her heart was lost while he kept his.

And she hated it. For a second hated him with the same passion with which she wanted him, with which she loved him. That he could be so coolly lucid at a moment so sublime stopped her from saying more.

She hoped he had no idea what was on the tip of her tongue. No clue as to what she longed to say to him. She was a fool.

Emotionally she tried to close off but couldn't. He wouldn't let her. With his kisses and touches he teased her until she could no longer think, could no longer hide behind any barriers she thought she'd built.

'Please, please, please!' She wasn't begging for just physical fulfilment. She wanted more, wishing that this weren't a mere casual affair.

He could make her feel so good. She wanted him to like her, wanted to be his equal—in every way. And she wasn't. She had to shut the door on the flow of love from her heart to his—she couldn't give it all to him. Not when she wouldn't get it back. He'd never give it back to her.

In the end she was forced to forget her doubts, to swallow her declaration as her feelings took over. She wouldn't utter the words, but she couldn't stop the response of her body. She gave in to the demands of his, took the pleasure he offered. The cries of need were torn from her. The tears of heartbreak would fall later. She'd take the ecstasy now and cope with the empty aftermath when he was gone.

But for once her scream of release was silent.

For a long time he lay on top, still joined with her, his heavy weight pressing her into the mattress, his breath hot on her neck. She didn't mind; she'd miss it terribly later. She rested her cheek on the pillow and blinked, not wanting him to see any hint of her weakness. Now, more than ever, she had to keep up the party front. But tiredness stripped her of all protection, all defence.

He lifted his head, took her chin in his hand and turned her face so she was looking straight up at him—there was no way to avoid the intense scrutiny. She held her breath and tried to hide chaos within. She tried to cover the need in her eyes, the love and longing.

But despite her attempt there must have been something in her face that he didn't want to see because his expression hardened and the veils across his eyes were thicker than she could ever hope hers could be. He let go of her chin, and eased off her. He pushed her gently, rolling her to the side, and fitted his body behind hers in a snug, warm embrace, but one in which she could no longer see his face. And he could no longer see hers.

'You need to get some sleep.' A slightly rough command. He rubbed his hand down her back, slow smooth strokes that were firm yet relaxing. And with each sweep her anxiety lessened and the tiredness increased. Until all her energy to fight and to fret was gone. She closed her eyes. Almost asleep she felt him move, felt the coldness as he left the bed and she wanted to call him back.

She must have done, because after a moment his weight depressed the bed again. She tried to stay awake, to pretend to sleep so she could savour it, but later, when she tried to remember, she couldn't be sure how long he sat—or indeed if she'd just dreamt it—leaning over her, stroking her hair from her forehead with such a gentle hand.

She jerked upright, heart thundering as consciousness returned and with it all the worry. What the *hell* was she doing *sleeping*? This was her last night to find someone—anyone—to organise some music. She glanced at her watch—it was just before nine. Panic set in—she'd spend all night tracking someone down if she had to, it was fundamental for the success of the party. She pulled on some clothes—her usual club outfit of slim dress and strappy sandals.

James was standing, staring out of the window, hair rumpled. A quick glance showed a half-empty takeaway container beside his laptop on the desk. He turned as she wandered into the room, looked surprised. 'I thought you were asleep for the night.'

'I need to work on some things.' She flicked a comb through her hair and gave thanks for straightening irons— they worked wonders in moments.

He took a step towards her. 'Do you need some help? Is there anything I can do?'

She didn't want him to soften up now. What had he seen this afternoon in bed? What had he read in her face? She knew he was reaching out to her, but she had to block him—for now anyway. 'You set me the challenge, James. Let me finish it.'

He frowned. 'You're sure you're managing OK? You still look tired.'

There was more than one reason why she was tired. She pinned on a bright smile. 'I'm without my make-up.'

He looked sceptical. 'I've seen you freshly scrubbed and wearing nothing but steam. It's not the lack of make-up.'

No. She was beyond beat. But she refused to give up now. She wanted to do it. She'd been burning to prove something to everyone for so long and she was so close to clinching this. If she could just work out this last detail, she'd have done it. Then maybe James truly would see more in her—maybe she'd let him. If she could prove to him first that she wasn't totally unreliable, that he could believe in her, she could relax and let her guard down. Maybe, if she did that, he might want her to stick around.

'I've got a few last-minute details to check. I'll see you later.' She blew him a kiss and got to the door before he had a chance to say or do much to stop her. She had to get on with the job—but she was fast running out of options and didn't know where next to turn.

James lay, half awake, half dreaming of his pleasure princess. He imagined her lying next to him, deep in sleep, her arms stretched above her head as she so often had them, utterly exposed to him, utterly relaxed. His fingers itched to touch her warm skin, to feel her softness. In the dark, waiting for her return, he admitted how much he'd been enjoying this week. Having her so close to him—having her as his. His blood, his emotions, everything seemed to be pumping nearer to the surface. He felt more alive than ever—and more attracted than ever. It wasn't just the magnificent sex they had together, but it was her—her company, her conversation, her laughter.

But this afternoon she'd come in with no laughter—looking tired, and pale and lonely. And she'd clung to him, her mouth seeking, hungry for more than just sex. And after, he'd looked deep into her eyes and she'd seemed to be offering a whole lot more than he'd ever expected. More than he'd ever thought he'd want.

It had shaken him. Because he suddenly realised he did want it.

The attraction wasn't going away. Every moment they had together he wanted ten more—twenty, a million. He had to work out how he was going to get himself out of this without getting hurt. But he was starting to hope that maybe he wouldn't have to.

She was snippy and smart and sometimes sullen, but she was also sweet and sexy and generous—and seeking something more from life. He knew she was and he badly wanted to believe she was loyal. She'd been working hard this week—really making the effort and he wanted to help her. Maybe he'd been wrong—maybe she was different. But as hope filled him self-mockery soared too. Uncertainty sucked.

He rolled, stretched across the bed, too tired to be able to work it out. He just wanted her to come home to him soon. Lay for hours half dozing before finally tumbling into sleep.

* * *

He woke early, alone and grouchy. Not even a triple-strength coffee and a chocolate apricot Danish helped shake the grouch. There was no sign of her return—no shoes flung in the far corner, no glass on the bench from a late-night drink of water. And he refused to knock on the door to see if she was in the other bedroom. Doubt started to gnaw.

He flicked on his computer. Might as well clear emails and check the headlines. He went to the usual pages and then checked out the local newspaper's site—wanting to see if there was a piece about the party tonight.

The photo showed her blurry, stumbling out of a club. She had a hand outstretched, grabbing onto the arm of the guy by her side.

Princess Elissa looking much the worse for wear. Back on Aristo for a week, it hasn't taken long for her to get back to her partying ways. Looking uncharacteristically pale, she embarked on a punishing party schedule that saw her at three different clubs through the night…

Last night? He quickly read it through again, checked out the digital clock on the side of the picture—showing time and date. Yes. Last night.

There was another picture pasted alongside—outside another club—and then there was another—taken *earlier in the week*? But she'd been with him all night, every night, hadn't she?

Hell. He thought for a while and realised he couldn't actually be certain. He'd been sleeping like the dead for the few hours he was in bed. Mentally beat from work and physically worn from all the intimacy with Elissa. Emotionally he was exhausted.

He swore, short and sharp. She could have gone. Of *course* she'd gone.

The spectre of betrayal had him scorching hot in a flash. Hadn't he been enough for her? What the hell did the woman want?

Anger exploded within him. *Idiot.* He had known. He'd warned himself all along. Hadn't he? Here he'd been thinking she was tired from trying to pull together this party. He'd been dreaming she wanted more from him. Actually imagining that she was falling for him. He'd laugh if it weren't so awful. What a damn, naïve bloody fool he was. *Again.*

She was tired because she'd been up all night partying. Who had she been dancing with—had she gone fresh from his arms into someone else's? Bitterness flooded his body—making him move. He had to do something. He paced as memories and pain tore at him. Why did this happen? Why were the women in his life so disloyal? He stopped walking, tried to claw back some strength. He'd been here before; he'd get through it again.

A second later, he was striding again. This time it was worse. This time it was a thousand times worse. Jenny had been all humiliation—her betrayal had been so public, so blithe. And he'd been so blind.

This was pure hurt. Nothing but hurt. He found he didn't care about other people knowing. All that mattered was that she had gone.

He ran both hands through his hair, clenched his hands and pulled—wanting the slight physical pain to distract him from the agony within. It shouldn't be as painful as this. It shouldn't feel as if she'd stuck white-hot swords through him on every side.

As he paced the room, breathing hard, the vitriol ran through his veins. She was a bitch, a vain-hearted bitch with an insatiable need to be adored by many. With no understanding of love or loyalty—no capacity to truly, deeply care. Why had he been fool enough to want to believe in her? How could he have let hormones interfere with his heart? How could he honestly have started to believe, to hope that she was different?

The door opened. He whirled around from where he was mid-flight back across the floor. She was still wearing last night's outfit. The outfit she'd been snapped in several times at several clubs—making an exhibition of herself.

'Did you have a good time?' he snapped, moving towards her.

Wariness sprang into her eyes.

He didn't need to ask any more. He couldn't stop himself. 'You look pale. Got a headache?'

'Actually—'

'Of course you do. Must be a mighty hangover if you got so drunk you were falling over outside that club.'

She stared.

'Take a look at the picture, princess.' He pointed to the laptop. 'Little ugly, isn't it? For someone so vain I'm surprised you let yourself be caught like that.'

He glared at her, incensed by the surprise on her face as she saw the pictures plastered over the Internet. 'What, you thought you'd get away with it? That I wouldn't find out?' He laughed; it felt rough and tasted acrid. 'I can't believe I thought you were taking this seriously. That you were looking tired from actually doing some work for once in your life. But you haven't, have you? Instead you've been sneaking out to go clubbing like some sixteen-year-old brat.'

'I—'

'You've been out other nights too, haven't you?'

Silently she nodded.

'Can't you bear to miss even a week out of the scene?' he bitterly jibed. 'The party is *tonight*, Liss. Or had you forgotten that?'

'I hadn't forgotten.'

'When that's over, this whole thing is over.' And he couldn't wait to forget all of it. Every last damn minute, every soft sigh, every silken touch—he'd expunge the lot. But right now rage burned. 'I thought there was more to you, Elissa. I wanted there to be more. But you really are just that shallow, spoilt kid.'

Liss had a headache all right, and it was thumping. She was tired, she'd been traipsing round club to club last night trying to find someone half decent to spin some tunes at the party. At some hellish new club she'd found some scary-looking guy who she'd made swear not to play anything too tuneless, too loud or too boring. She'd had no sleep because when she'd finally got back to the hotel she'd spent the last few hours in the office downstairs typing up the rest of the brochure for the media kit. What did he *think* she'd been up to? The accusation in his eyes had her hackles on end.

'Where have you been?' He couldn't seem to leave it alone.

She finally got the chance to get a whole answer in. 'Are you able to believe me if I tell you?'

His face tightened and her heart sank.

'I'm not going to tell you when there is no point. You've already condemned me.' Based on nothing, he was so obviously thinking the worst. 'I thought you were just, James. I thought you were the kind of guy who could give someone a chance. A second chance even.' She looked for some kind of response, but he didn't give an inch, still stood with anger carved into him. 'And in the workplace, it seems you can. But not personally. You've given me no chance, no chance at all.'

She didn't try to defend herself further. Why bother? So much for thinking he'd seen more in her. So much for worrying that that meant he'd guessed how she really felt about him. Why had she thought he'd see past her act? And why had she been so stupid as to secretly wish he had?

'Why should I? It's obvious. You're as flighty and self-centred as they come.'

'If that's what you think, James,' she answered tiredly.

'What else is there to think?'

If he couldn't see any other reason for her actions, then too bad. At least now she knew exactly where she stood.

Alone.

CHAPTER THIRTEEN

LISS spent the morning supervising the final decoration of the ballroom. It took several hours to get the tapestries hung right, but the lights were in place, the chef and his team were having a frantic but fun time. It didn't seem possible, but it was actually going to come together. The dodgy DJ showed up and set up his equipment and all she could do was cross her fingers and hope that he wouldn't play anything too awful.

Tino dropped the dress to her just after lunch. She slipped into it, amazed at how well he'd made it to fit—despite only working from her measurements. It was incredible. And for the minutes she had it on, she felt incredible.

'You're very talented,' she said, twisting to look at the back in the mirror. 'When I can I'll be ordering some more dresses from you. But I bet I'll be joining an ever-expanding queue. Where did you get this fabric?' She made pleasantries—anything to take her mind off James.

'Bahrain. Cost a bomb and I've been hanging on to it for ages—too scared to put scissors anywhere near it.' Tino's grin was shaky, a rare indication of nerves. 'But I think it's worth it for this dress. Stunning, isn't it?'

'It's so soft.' The silk warmed against her skin, but felt so light, as if she were draped in tissue paper. As delicate and fragile as she felt inside. 'How are the crew looking?' She stood statue-still as he went to sew a minor alteration.

'Damn hot,' he replied, swaggering once more with confidence. 'Stella's downstairs overseeing hair and make-up.'

Liss managed a smile, fervently hoping he was right and they were the ultimate in glam serving staff. But if the dress he'd made for her was anything to go by, she was in the clear.

'I really appreciate all the work you've done.'

He stood back and scrutinised her with the clinical eye of the professional. 'You're going to knock them dead.'

She smiled, hoped he was right on that front too. But there was only one person on her hit list. 'You would say that—it's your design.'

'That only a figure like yours can pull off. Thanks for the opportunity, princess.'

He turned away while she slipped out of the dress and into her robe. 'Thank you. You've helped me out much more than you realise.'

After carefully hanging the dress in the wardrobe, she walked him to the door of her bedroom. For a moment they stood chatting, him just outside the door, her leaning against the jamb.

'I'll be sure to tell every journalist I see who designed the dress.'

'Excellent.'

'Make sure you enjoy the party.'

'You too, princess. You should get some rest now. I didn't design that dress for it to be worn with bags.'

He tapped below his eyes with a finger.

Of course James had to walk in just then. Dressed in a suit

but looking as if he'd been through a storm—his tie askew, his hair ruffled, his jaw stubbled, his eyes burning.

Liss froze, felt incredibly conscious that she was wearing only her robe. She felt more naked than she ever had—even when literally naked and intimate in bed with him. And still, despite her vulnerability, he didn't see her—not as she really was. He saw no innocence in her or in the situation.

She didn't need to be a rocket scientist to figure out what he was thinking—the worst. So it was official—he only ever thought the worst. Just like all of them. All he saw was a vacuous party girl with nothing more to offer than a short-lived good time—and offering it to anyone. No matter what happened tonight, no matter how successful the ball was, he'd never see her as anything more.

His stare was scathing, raking over both her and Tino as he strode past, straight into his room. The door slammed.

Tino looked at her with raised brows.

'Sorry about that,' Liss said, but made no more excuses, simply showing him out with as polite a smile as she could manage. She'd just shut the door on him when James's opened again.

'Who was that?' Straight to it, a lethal bullet.

'Why?'

'I just want to know.'

She walked forward with calm steps that were utterly at odds with the mad beat of her heart and the dread dancing in her stomach. 'You don't trust me, do you, James?'

Silence. Her body was washed through with bitter disappointment. She could see the fever in his eyes, the way it was eating him up. He wasn't capable of listening right now and she was too hurt by it and too tired to fight—to make him see sense. So instead, she decided to tell him his own truth.

'You see only what you choose to see. And what you choose destroys anything we have together. Is that really what you want?'

He wouldn't trust her. Refused to. She couldn't understand why—what had she done to make him doubt her like this?

All her secret hopes and dreams died. If he didn't trust her, he could never love her.

His glare burnt into her, hard, glowing. His jaw set and his mouth barely moved as he ground the words out. 'I don't want anything from *you*.' He looked away then, his eyes seeming blind as he strode back into his room.

The door slammed louder that time.

Shaken, she silently went into her own room. His rage had been a visible, living thing, but he'd told her everything he needed to in one pithy sentence. She leaned back against the door, her fist pressed to her side as if trying to stop the internal haemorrhage.

Eventually, many deep breaths later, she managed to transform the hurt into a rod of cold steel. She inserted it down her spine. He might say that, but she knew better. He had wanted her and if he was honest he still wanted her. He just didn't see all that she was. Well, she wasn't just some plaything— not any more. She could achieve, had achieved, would achieve more. Whether he chose to acknowledge it or not, she told herself not to care. Impossible of course, but she'd try anyway.

She'd go out there tonight, be proud of what she'd pulled together and hold her head high. James Black be damned.

In the shower she let herself have a moment—just one moment—when hot tears fell unchecked, scalding her cheeks, and the ache in her throat pierced her as she choked back the howl of agony. For just that time she let the break in her heart be fully felt.

Then she locked it away, wishing she had an impenetrable chest—had never known it was possible to feel pain this way. She was just going to have to lock it away for ever; it hurt too badly. Then she made the tears stop and the thoughts be buried. She lay on the bed and blanked everything from her mind. She was not going to go to the ball with red, blotchy cheeks. No man was worth that.

James steered clear of the hotel all the late afternoon. His manager could show the media around. He only needed to be there for the ball and could get away with a brief chat to them then.

The anger wouldn't go away. The hurt underneath it only seemed to be growing. He wished he'd yelled. He wished she'd yelled back. Wished she'd told him exactly what she'd been doing and made him look a fool.

But she'd refused. And thus must be guilty. But now, stupidly, *he* felt guilty. She'd made him feel as if he were the one in the wrong—that typical womanly way of twisting things: fickle with the truth.

He'd just wanted to know.

Glancing at his watch, he realised he was going to have to race to get ready on time. He hadn't achieved anywhere near as much as he'd wanted to. Tried to focus on business elsewhere but his thoughts were scattered and staying on task proved impossible.

He ran the blade down his jaw with quick, sure strokes. Stepped into his tux almost straight from the steaming shower, his hair still damp. After tying his shoes he took a quick look in the mirror to check everything was in the right place. And for the first time all week didn't bother putting a condom or three into his pocket. That madness was finished.

Another look at his watch and he walked through to the lounge. Allowed himself to think of her since that moment in there when it had felt as if his guts had been ripped from his body. The guy had been dressed in jeans and looked dishevelled and exhausted—as if he'd been up all night.

She'd looked exhausted too—pale with blue-tinged rings under her eyes. James winced. He already knew she'd been up all night—just not with him.

Where she was now, he had no idea. Who she was with— no idea either. And even if the effort was going to kill him, he was going to train himself not to care.

She couldn't make too much of a mess of the evening. The hotel itself was a masterpiece. There was wine, there was food. A little music and some chat and it would be OK. Perhaps not the incredible success he'd envisaged, but he'd cope. The sooner he got off this island, the better. He'd assign his next-in-command to take care of it from now on.

He went to the little table by the door where the staff left the paper and any mail for them—and where he usually left his keycard. There was some mail there and he glanced at it. It only took a second to realise it wasn't for him, but in fact was mail that Liss had written and had put there to be sent. A postcard, writing side up, and he couldn't stop himself reading part of it. Addressed to Atlanta House, it said how exciting it was that Sandy had given birth to a beautiful daughter and how she couldn't wait to meet her. She passed on her love and best wishes to the other girls and said she'd be in touch again soon. James pushed the postcard to the side. The warmth so evident in the writing attacked his certainty. Only there was another postcard beneath it, also writing side up, and the address took only a second to scan—to the youthline in Paris. He didn't read the whole thing, didn't need to. It was clearly a full-of-chat-and-questions card to the other volunteers who worked there. James blinked. So she still kept in touch with them too?

Beside the cards there was a small wooden toy—with a tag proudly declaring it had been 'Handcrafted in Aristo'. It sat on top of an envelope. He nudged the toy. The envelope was addressed to Sandy, care of Atlanta House. The gesture bit into him. It was a sweet thing to do, and he didn't want to think of her as sweet right now.

He stared at the little rattle for a while, awash with conflicting feelings. Then it dawned on him that he had no idea what he was supposed to be doing. Was he supposed to be greeting guests already? Gritting his teeth, he supposed he'd better go to the ballroom and find out what she'd come up with.

And even though he told himself he didn't care, with every step towards the room his muscles tightened further.

In the doorway he stopped.

It wasn't anything like he'd imagined. No one could ever have imagined this—except Liss. Bitter pride twisted through him tornado style.

She'd done it.

One side of the room was walled with people—the media, all in attendance this time, just as he'd wanted. And their focus was on one thing and one thing only.

She stood in the centre of the ballroom, speaking—he had no idea what she was saying. Only one of his senses was working—sight. She was wearing one hell of a dress. The straps rested almost on the very edge of her shoulders, emphasising her collarbones. His thumb itched to rest below the ridge of the bone, fingers wanted to slide above and along the slim length. He already knew how it felt—smooth and fine but strong too.

The neckline dropped low, a wide vee down her cleavage. In turn this emphasised the way her body curved in so tight at the waist. Her hips were slimmer—not as broad as her shoulders but still a beautiful, graceful curve. From there the material tumbled to the floor in a golden cascade.

He didn't know what the fabric was. But it was as if it were alive. With a gentle shimmer, it clung to and floated from her slender figure.

He frowned—her slightly *too* slender figure.

She looked so incredibly regal—and suddenly way out of his league. She spoke again and he heard her that time.

'Pack away your cameras, people. And prepare to party.'

Not a single camera was lowered. Rather the shutters kept opening and closing quickly—capturing the country's favourite young princess in full royal mode.

She nodded her head at a waiter standing near the service doors and he swung them open. Incredible-looking wait staff filed in—one line of men, one of women. James recognised some of them from the other night but most he didn't. And they were gorgeous. The women's hair had been tied up at the front with the length trailing down their backs. With figure-hugging white tops, white skirts that were slim over the waist and hips but then flared out, ending just at the knee. Then it was all legs and arched feet in barely there, flimsy-heeled sandals of the kind Liss would adore. The simple look of golden tanned skin was shown to advantage by the crisp, clean white and highlighted by lengths of gold ribbon which had been wound round their figures—emphasising sensual curves and slender waists.

Every single one was gorgeous and each made that simple look sexy. They might be wearing white, but not one of them looked as if their thoughts were completely pure. Glittering make-up added to the glamour factor.

It took him a minute to really notice the men, but they, like the women, carried trays of glasses filled with some concoction. Only instead of white they wore black. Close-fitting tops and immaculate trousers. All clean-shaven, short-haired and a smouldering look in their eyes. Looking like the servants of night, they too seemed to be offering something more than a simple drink.

They were all covered, there was nothing blatant—no bare boobs or hairy chests—yet there was something so sensual, so sexual about the group of beautiful young men and women lined up to serve. Nymphs and Satyrs.

And in the centre of them all stood Liss, resplendent in the golden dress. Unlike the others all of her hair was swept up high, curls on her head were like a crown showing off her height, the luscious length of her neck.

From the walls hung huge tapestries with the scenes of what appeared to be Greek myths—rich and fascinating and, from what he could see, slightly naughty.

With the tapestries behind her, and the burnished gold glow that seemed to come from nowhere but that shrouded the place with a warm intimate hue, she was the golden rose.

Like a tableau they stood—Aphrodite with her attendants. A scene from Greek mythology lifted into the modern-day world.

The photographers kept popping their heads up from behind the lenses as if to check what they were seeing was real. James could hardly believe it himself.

She stood still for a moment longer, the smile of Venus on her lips. She could have been one of the world's great models if she'd wanted to. He'd never seen a more beautiful woman. And the question vexed him—was her beauty all on the outside, or the inside? What was it that made her so beautiful? Her eyes, her skin, her hair, her smile? Or was it the bubbly personality and spirit of generosity? Her natural, calm elegance came with a touch of mischief, of love, of laughter and fun. So irresistible.

And how was it that she could stand here in front of the world and there was no hint of that blush? Surely she must be feeling self-conscious? Who wouldn't? But thinking on it, he'd only ever seen that blush when right up close to her. When *he* was right up close to her.

She turned then, and he forgot everything. The dress was a masterpiece, but only a foil to the body beneath. Aside from two very long, very thin straps, there was no back to her dress. Only smooth, golden skin revealed. The material started again fractionally above where the curve of her bottom began. James, like every male in the room, was transfixed.

After a second's pause in which everyone in the room took a collective breath, the frenzy of camera clicks started again.

Seeming to ignore it, Elissa nodded and the waiting staff moved towards the media pack, offering them the drinks. Then she turned back to face the line-up.

'The other guests will soon be arriving. If you want to catch them on the red carpet outside, now is your chance to get your spot. Otherwise you can remain here and start the party.'

But they wouldn't let her go—questions came at her from all directions.

'How do you like Sydney?'

'Will you be coming back to Aristo to live or is Australia your new home?'

'Who designed your dress, Elissa?'

James noticed the slight set to her smile under the on-slaught—the first hint of tension she'd let slip and so slight he doubted anyone else would even notice. But he was tuned in to every nuance of her body and expression and he read strain there. She chose to answer the third question.

'Tino Dranias, a young Aristan designer.' She gestured with her hand and a man walked past James; he hadn't realised there was anyone behind him. 'His work is just wonderful. If you think it looks nice, let me tell you it feels even better on.'

It was the man from the lounge. The one looking as if he'd been up all night. Of course he had—hunched over a sewing machine. James could taste the humble pie already.

'Tino styled the wait staff tonight too.' The young designer looked pretty blown away as he smiled into the lenses of over a hundred cameras.

Liss looked as if she'd been doing it all her life—and she had, of course. But still, she had such grace under pressure.

'What about Australia, Elissa? Is that your new home now?'

The flash in her eyes wouldn't have been noticed by any of them. Or if it had they couldn't have interpreted it. But James had seen that look before, when he'd asked her to name one thing she wanted that she didn't have.

'I'm enjoying Sydney but I'll probably move on again soon. I'm not ready to settle into anywhere for long yet.' Her answer was delivered with the flippant lilt he'd heard often before. But there was an off note in there. She was lying. He was sure of it.

Half the photographers scrummed out to where many paparazzi were already in place to catch the arrival of the guests, while the others remained, snapping the room, the waiters, still trying to get a word from Liss. She moved quickly though, pausing by James on her way. A quick, low mutter in his ear. 'I know it's not all about me, James, but they wanted photos and I thought it might help.'

Hell, yes, it helped. But she wouldn't meet his eyes and he needed to make contact with her—some sort of communication that could carry them through the evening to a time when they could really talk. A compliment might help.

'You look beautiful. Like Aphrodite.'

That earned him a quick look—one that stabbed. 'Aphrodite was a vain and selfish creature who cheated on her husband.'

Wrong choice, then. His feeling of guilt trebled.

'Liss, I—'

'Better go mingle.'

She turned, smiling keenly into the crowd, and didn't glance his way again.

The sensation that she was wrong—that he'd been wrong—grew. It *was* all about her. Everything he was feeling was all about her. And he had to make it right.

Ironically he regretted the media presence. She was keenly aware of them, as was he, and it meant he couldn't get within any sort of distance—certainly not nearly as close as he'd like.

He lifted a glass from one of the nymphettes' trays, grimaced weakly at her bright-eyed beauty and decided to get the duty bit out of the way. So he talked to a few of the journalists; they all gushed about the tour they'd been on.

'And your room is satisfactory?' Mr Suave Hotel Magnate himself.

'The most amazing view actually.'

Coming from this hardened hack it was some compliment and James knew he had no need to worry about what the reports were going to be like in the papers, magazines and TV shows over the next week.

Liss hadn't just invited the sycophants. She'd invited some cynics as well. And she'd won them over.

Of course it wasn't all down to her. The hotel was beautiful, with a fabulous location and outlook. No detail had been spared and whatever the hell they were drinking it tasted damned nice. But without the X-factor of Princess Elissa, the night wouldn't have been nearly such a success.

'Have you got all the information you need?'

The guy flashed a little booklet. 'Press pack from our princess has all the info necessary.'

'Good.' James itched to grab it off him and see what she had written.

But now the journalist was looking over to where Liss stood encircled by several guests. 'She does the decorative bit well, doesn't she? Still, I guess it's easy when you've never had to do a decent day's work in your life.'

James paused. Not so much suave but stiff now. 'On the contrary, Princess Elissa works very hard at both her job and her charity work.'

The hack turned to James, cynical laughter deepening the lines etched into his face. 'Princess Elissa doesn't *do* any charity work.'

James stared at the journalist—then saw his own astonishment reflected as the other man's expression changed. He clamped his jaw shut and stared him out, deciding not to argue as he saw the million questions leap in the journalist's eyes. The guy was practically sniffing the air for the story. He opened his mouth, but James got in first, murmuring tightly, 'Please excuse me, I must see to something.'

James left the ballroom, needing a second to steer clear of journalists and reorder his thoughts, which were suddenly going chaotic—no one knew about her visits? Her volunteering? It wasn't all for show?

Breathing hard, he found a stack of spare press packs out by Reception. Opening one, he saw it included brochures on the other hotels in the chain as well as a small leaflet about tonight's event. It listed details of what was being served, the key players in the hotel chain—including his business bio. He flicked through the service listings—the dress designer's contact details were there, the lighting guy, the DJ. Apparently the additional waiting staff were courtesy of Ellos Modelling Agency. That explained all the beauties, then.

It got him thinking. She must have put in some hours getting this together—*all* hours. God, he was an idiot.

Here he was thinking she hadn't been taking it seriously, had just been partying on. Instead she'd been incredibly focused and incredibly productive.

What else had she been taking seriously? What about him? Had she been taking their affair seriously too?

He hadn't. Quite the opposite, in fact. Right from the start he'd pigeonholed her and based on what? The bitter lens that Jenny had left him with—the warped one. He blinked, refocused and thought—really *thought* about how things were. The way she'd persevered even when she was so completely hopeless at typing; the effort she'd made with those girls at Atlanta House; those nights in Sydney when he'd watched from his apartment as she'd come home—always alone and not once stumbling in her ridiculous shoes; the way she took him so completely into her—giving everything, wanting to give him maximum pleasure every time. The bad feeling inside simply grew.

He went back to the ball. For a while he did more watching than participating. Cynically studied the socialites and dignitaries and their love-hate relationship with press hounds and paparazzi. Tonight was a love night. They greeted each other, most having encountered many times in the past, with smiles and air kisses and the occasional camera click. It was a night for courting, and photos of 'my best side' and time to forget uglier scenes of thrown punches and non-molestation orders.

But there were press people here who were celebrities in their own right, world-famous photographers for whom even the most publicity-shy superstar would beg to sit. It was an incredible line-up. And under the rich tapestries and sublime lighting, they all seemed to glow. It wasn't just her contacts that made it a success, but the ambience she'd created.

And he'd ruined it—for her and for him. He knew she was hiding her hurt. With one moment of absolute rabid-dog madness he'd severed their connection. Jealousy, he reflected, was an insidious, hideous thing and insecurity utterly destructive.

He hadn't been fair. He, who prided himself on being just that, on giving people the chance to prove their worth, hadn't been fair to her at all. Sure, he'd given her chance after chance professionally. But personally? Not one. Just as she'd said.

He'd only been willing to believe the worst—*wanting* to believe the worst. She'd been right about that too—it was what he'd wanted to see. And why? Because it was a convenient out. He'd allowed the past to blind him. Because he'd felt scared. It had been the most cowardly moment of his life.

Fact was, Princess Elissa Karedes scared him to death. Or, rather, the feelings he had for her did. For those mad moments he'd wanted to believe the worst of her because he didn't want to let himself be in love with her.

He didn't want to be hurt.

It was too late—for either of those things.

The hours dragged. He hadn't gone near her all evening because when he did he didn't want anyone else around. What was going to happen between them was utterly private. This was her moment in the sun. The party had been such a success and he knew the media coverage would be good—he wasn't about to blow all her hard work on creating a bigger ripple than the king and the palace maid rumour. And if he got closer than five feet to her right now, there'd be one hell of a scandal.

Seeing her across the room, he knew the effort she'd put in—her integrity was obvious. She glowed with the self-belief, the pride, the dignity in a job well done.

The self-hatred, the humiliation and the hurt in having screwed up something far more important ate into him.

Damn the press. He had to move, had to fight—he knew now it was his life on the line.

CHAPTER FOURTEEN

Liss worked the party and smiled more than she'd ever smiled in her life. Worked hard to appear happy on the outside when on the inside she was totally torn apart. James had hardly said a word to her all evening. She'd turned away from him right at the start and he hadn't been near since.

And she was tired. She didn't want to see the party through to its final moment—even though she knew it was a success. While one part of her could almost celebrate, the rest of her just wanted to run away and let her broken heart bleed openly. She faced the fact it was going to be at least another couple of hours before that could happen and mentally squared her shoulders. She'd discovered the depth of her own strength this last week. She just hoped she'd never have to use it again. Right now she'd go once more into the social round.

He caught her just as she was about to join another group. Took her elbow and turned her away from the others. Her whole arm sizzled and at his fierce expression her heart broke all over again.

'I was going to wait until the end of the evening to talk to you.' He spoke low in her ear. 'But I find I can't. Can we have a quick meeting now?'

She nodded, not wanting to, but not wanting a public scene. She walked with him, down the corridor back to the suite of meeting rooms. He ushered her into one and locked the door behind them. The same damn room as last week. She moved into the middle of it; he followed. She wouldn't look up at him, not wanting to see the cold condemnation she was sure would be there. What had she done wrong this time?

'The guy coming out of your room was the dress designer, wasn't he?'

Her vision splintered. She didn't want to go over this. Didn't want him to drag her through the barbs once more. But she nodded, couldn't trust her voice not to break.

'I saw him at the photo shoot you had. I figure he's probably gay.'

'He's not gay.' It was a whisper. She wished she could get some kind of perverse pleasure from telling him that, but all she felt was hurt.

'No? But he's not your type anyway, is he?'

She shook her head. He should know that.

'Am I your type, Liss?'

She froze, knotted her hands together as her skin ran both hot and cold. 'I don't want to talk about that…' The words rushed out, and then she rushed too, pushing past him, wanting to get away.

He grabbed her mid-flight, his fingers clenching on her upper arms as he pulled her towards him. 'I'm sorry.' The words flew rough and hard. His hands gripped harder. 'I'm sorry.'

She stopped, kept her head low. All she could see was the white of his shirt jerking across his chest. His fingers loosened just a little.

'Listen to me,' he said fiercely. Then he breathed for a bit. 'Please.'

She didn't reply, but didn't try to pull away either. What was he sorry for? What did he want to say to her? She could hardly hear for the hope and the fear thundering in her ears.

It was another moment before he spoke again. Then it came out, slow, quiet. 'You once asked if my mum and I had fallen out. We had—big time in a never-talk-about-it kind of way. It happened the day I came home from school early and found her at home with her lover. She was having an affair, right under my father's nose, jeopardising our whole family.' He spoke faster. 'She knew I knew. But it didn't end. And after a while I figured out it hadn't been the only one. Nor was it the last.' His bitterness was palpable as he paused. 'I've never told anybody that, Liss. Not even him.'

Stunned, Liss looked up. As she looked at the torment in his eyes her heart ached for the boy he'd been—for his loss of innocence and the burden he must have felt.

'I was so angry with him for not noticing. How could he not have known? And I was determined no woman would ever make a fool of me the way my mother had my dad.'

He grimaced. And Liss's heart sank lower when she saw the self-mockery in his eyes. Oh, no. She lifted her hands, placing them on his chest, wanting to support him.

His gaze dropped, but he kept talking. 'A couple of years ago I was in a serious relationship. Jenny was popular, a social butterfly, loved attention. What I didn't know was that behind my back she was screwing around. She got lazy with the latest and pictures of them together were published in the gossip mags. The rest of the world knew before I did—and the media revelled in it.'

Liss flinched. Opened her mouth, but he started talking again, even faster, and she couldn't interrupt, wanting to understand so badly.

'I refused to be hurt like that again, or so humiliated. I decided I was never getting serious with a woman, I'd just have the odd fling when the opportunity arose. And certainly I wasn't going to get involved with another butterfly type.'

He looked at her then, stormy apology heavy in his eyes. 'And then you waltzed in—so beautiful and so vivacious and so fun-loving.' He shook his head. 'I tried really hard not to like you, Liss. I told myself you were shallow and vain and wouldn't know the meaning of loyalty even if it bit you. But every step along the way you were showing me different. And I couldn't help but touch you and once I'd touched I couldn't stop and then every time I did, I wanted to explore more. I wanted to understand you.'

He broke off for a moment and then changed tack. 'And you attract all this bloody attention. Except for promoting my hotels, I hate the press thing, Liss.' He sighed. 'But you were sweet and generous and blindly searching for something and all I wanted to do was help you.' He paused, his intensity mounting. 'And have you. But when I thought you'd left me asleep in bed and gone clubbing? I felt like such a naïve fool. And I thought you'd done everything I feared the most. That moment was worse than anything—worse than Mum, worse than Jenny. And I lost it. I totally lost it.'

Inside the pain sharpened—pain for him, pain for herself, and she whispered, 'Have I ever given you reason not to trust *me*?' Tears filled her eyes so fast they burned.

He paled. 'No. I know it was unfair of me. I've been unfair all along. I wanted out, Liss. It was going to be an affair on Aristo and then all over.' He shook as he breathed in and his fingers dug tight into her arms again. 'But I can't.' He pulled her closer and the strain cracked his voice. 'I can't let you go.'

The tears coursed down her face as she was submerged in hurt and longing. 'I don't want you to.' Her voice broke even harsher as her need sobbed out. 'I don't want you to *ever* let me go.'

Agonised and angry, she looked up at him, and saw desperate painful need reflected. And then his mouth came down on hers, grinding her lips against her teeth, crushing her as if he couldn't get close enough. His hands tightened even more, clamping her to him, and she struggled to get hers free—so she could throw her arms around his neck and cling on just as tight. She wanted to make it all better for him—for both of them. She wanted to love him and for him to let her.

They strained together, fighting to get close, until he took charge, backing her up against the wall fast because she could barely stand. Swiftly he ran his hands hard down her body and then swept her dress up; she caught at the fabric, wanting it out of the way but there was no time and it fluttered around them. His fingers ran up her thighs and as he discovered she was totally naked beneath the gold fabric he muttered something unintelligible, his whole body jerking as he flung forward.

'For you, James. Only for you,' she whispered. For him she was utterly bare. She spread her legs wider, pushing her hips away from the wall, eager for him to enter. He got his hand between them, ran his fingers in her cleft, hot and wet. As their mouths met and meshed she heard his zip and convulsed with the anticipation. She arched to meet him, watching his expression through half-lowered lids as the most intimate parts of their bodies pressed together. His teeth came down hard on his lip.

She stilled. There was something different. He stopped. His fingers squeezed hard on her thighs as he groaned. His eyes bored into hers, filled with agony. 'It's just me, Liss. I haven't got anything with me.'

No protection. No thin cover stopping her from totally

getting to know him. She could feel both the softness of his skin and the hardness of the muscle beneath. He was hers to take deep inside—to embrace wholly.

'Take a chance?' There was a note in his voice that she'd never heard before. The thin strain of vulnerability. The tiny chink revealing his weakness—that she was his weakness. Her heart swelled. Accepting him was a risk she couldn't not take.

'Oh, yes.'

They both pushed again and met together. She trembled with the sensation, heard his rough choke. Her breath hissed out, choppy, painful. He felt so fantastic. So raw.

She curled one leg around him, rising high on her toes to get the angle—so he could drive in as close and as tight as possible. His hands slid up her legs, holding and teasing and pushing the dress away. She couldn't look away from the emotion written so clearly on his face.

'Liss.' His eyes were golden brown pools—liquid and loving and so full of need it tore her apart and she could hide nothing from him.

It was the most erotic, most naked moment of her life.

He could hardly seem to speak, his words coming jerky, through clenched teeth. 'I'm trying really, really hard not to ruin your dress.'

'I don't care about the dress, just don't stop.' She took the material, lifted it higher.

'I don't know how gentle I can keep this.' The muscles in his jaw bunched.

'Just love me,' she begged.

His fingers clenched on her soft skin. Colour stained his cheekbones. A look of ecstatic agony crossed his face. Then he changed his grip, cupping her bottom, taking her weight and lifting her closer to him. He stared into her eyes, and his words came, quiet but clear. 'I do.'

With every strong stroke, he made her believe him. His eyes wouldn't leave hers, he just pushed closer and closer and closer and wouldn't let her look away, wouldn't let her hide from the truth that was so apparent in his uncontrollable reaction to her. And she sobbed as with every stroke he repeated the words—chanting them over and over. The intensity overwhelmed her, the taste of tears and love washing away the wounds of loneliness and the fear of loss.

She cried out from the force as wave after wave of unbearable pleasure hit. He held her, still surging forward, still strong as she collapsed about him. And then he thrust hard and deep, once, twice more, releasing everything into her. As his love poured in she closed her eyes and longed for it to take root and grow deep within.

His body pressed hers hard against the wall, swathes of material bunched between them. His forehead rested on her shoulder and she could feel his hot shuddering breaths on her chest. She stroked her hand through his hair, smoothing it, while the aftershocks still rippled through her own body.

'I don't want another day like today, Liss. I couldn't stand it.' The pain still echoed in his voice.

Liss placed her hands either side of his jaw, pushed gently so he lifted his head. She looked deep into his eyes. 'You have to trust me. Do you hear me? Because if you can't, then we won't work.'

Now she saw his vulnerability. That his mockery had been self-defence. He didn't need it—not with her.

'I want to but—'

'Don't you know what you've done for me?' She understood what he needed—the same as what she needed—reassurance and love. 'Don't you understand what you've done in my life?'

He blinked.

'You believed in me. You gave me chance after chance, you made me want to succeed at something. And I did. And it's all because of you.' She could never give him half as much as he'd given her. 'I may make mistakes, James, but I can promise you I'll never betray you.' He needed to understand that she'd sooner rip out her own heart than hurt his. 'I don't want to go to all those parties any more. Not unless you're there with me. I want normal things from life. I want a home, a family. I want you.' She stared into his eyes, willing him to believe her. 'I *love* you.'

For a moment he just stared back at her. Then he sighed, long and deep. The last of the tension drained from his features and he rested his forehead on hers and closed his eyes. 'Thank you.'

She ran her fingers down the side of his face, holding him tenderly, and wanting him to understand everything. 'When I went out the other night it was—'

'You don't need to tell me,' he butted in. 'I know there's no way you could have organised that party without working round the clock. You told me you were checking some details—I believe you.'

She smiled, but needed to explain anyway. 'I was trying to organise entertainment—a DJ or a band or something. It was such short notice and I had to find out if they were any good and if they could be released from the club for the evening. I didn't want to tell you. You were so busy, the last thing you needed was me adding to your list of things to do. I wanted to show you that I could do it, that I wasn't totally useless. I wanted to show you that you could believe in me. But none of my old friends would help me.' That rejection still stung. 'They didn't want to know.' She looked at him sadly. 'I guess they weren't really friends.'

She'd been dreaming for all these years, pretending, hiding from the truth. Now she could finally admit it. 'I've been so alone for so long, James.'

He slipped his arms right around her, cradled her to him. 'I know.'

She clung to him, feeling his warmth, and knew he could give her everything she hadn't had—family, friendship.

He stroked his hands down her back. 'I would have helped you.'

'I know.' And she did. 'I stumbled on my way out of the club and the paparazzi snapped the moment. For once my stupid shoes got me.'

'Your shoes aren't stupid,' he teased. 'They're the ultimate adornment for the most magnificent legs ever to walk the earth.'

She smiled but soon sobered, knowing there were still mountains for them to climb. 'They're always there, James— the paparazzi. It's just part of the deal. You just have to learn to ignore them and never read the papers.'

'How do you think they'll handle your wedding?'

'What?'

'Your marriage—will they be fighting for exclusive coverage?'

She stared, speechless.

His eyes sparkled with the golden flecks now. 'You might be the princess, but I'm still the boss. And I've decided the next event I want you to plan is our marriage. So long as you keep a tight rein on the budget and a close eye on the guest list, of course.' He winked.

'You want to marry me?' She knew he wanted her, that he loved her, but she hadn't expected that he'd ever want to take on such a public commitment. Not after what he'd been through, not with the sad example his parents had given him.

He tilted her chin and made her look at him. 'Your home is with me. My home is with you. *Permanently.*' His hand tightened on her waist. 'Understand?'

She was trying to, really trying. He wasn't going to let her go. He wasn't going to make her go. He *wanted* her. Just as she was, all that she was—for ever.

She couldn't believe it.

A smile, one more wry than wicked, softened the angles of his face. 'Is it bad of me to be hoping that I just got you pregnant? And if I didn't, then I'm going to keep trying till I do because then you'll *have* to marry me.'

'Oh, James.' Her eyes burned again.

'We'll have such fun with our kids, Liss.' His eyes glowed with the promise of heavenly dreams soon to be realised. 'We won't send them away either. No matter how wild they try to be.'

She crumpled then. He was offering her everything—her dream career, a family, a home, a heart that was all hers. All she'd ever wanted in the world, he wanted too. She clenched her fingers on his shoulders, keeping herself upright—just.

'No more tears.' He shook his head at her. 'You've ruined your make-up.'

'I don't give a damn about my make-up.' She hadn't slept in over twenty-four hours. She'd gone from the angst of uncertainty, to the despair of heartbreak, to the unending joy in knowing she now held the heart of her lover—unconditionally.

'Marry me.'

It was more of an order than a question but she didn't mind.
'Yes.'

Exhaustion disappeared in her elation and his expression exploded—excitement, relief, jubilance coloured him. He beamed, open and free, as she took his face in her hands and whispered with rapture yes, yes and yes to him again. He wiped the fresh tears from her cheeks with his thumbs, and then claimed his prize.

'We'd better get back to the bloody party.' He groaned, finally releasing her from a kiss that left them both breathless and needy. 'As soon as we can get away you can do your wild-child act for me.'

'Want me to striptease?' Oh, there would be nothing better than their own private party.

He laughed. 'It wouldn't take long, would it?'

She gave a saucy shimmy towards the door. 'I could do some dancing as well.'

His laughter slid into another groan. 'Don't torment me.'

Fingers linked, they left the room and walked back towards the ballroom. Just outside the double doors he stopped, turned. He snaked one arm around her waist and she leaned in, ready to receive and return the kiss.

With his thumb he stroked just under her collarbone, just above where her heart was beating. The tips of his fingers traced over the top of the bone. For a moment they paused, enjoying the moment of anticipation, of satisfaction, of pure happiness.

Then she heard the repeated clicking of a camera shutter close by.

She could feel the flush on her cheeks, the afterglow of love-making, knew her lips were swollen from kisses and that her eyes were probably as wide and revealing as James's were.

And she knew that one photographer had got his shot. *The* shot of the party. *The* story.

She relaxed and smiled back into James's resigned but still-smiling face. The clicking kept up.

They refrained from the kiss; it wasn't the kind of kiss to be done in public. But the look they shared would be read by the world.

Princess Elissa Karedes had found her safe harbour, her home. She had found her love.

* * * * *

Who will reunite the Stefani Diamond and rule Adamas?

*Housekeeper Effie has been claimed by the sheikh king—
for her innocence! But something will compel Zakari
to take her, a lowly servant, as his royal bride!*

Read on for an exclusive extract from the final book in
THE ROYAL HOUSE OF KAREDES *miniseries!*

SHE WAS SHAKING with nerves, yet still she was bold for him,
and that touched Zakari. His hands held her shoulders, his
eyes holding hers for the longest time—stunned at the magic
they had created this day and looking forward to the magic
they would create tonight.

And then his heart stopped.

Because there between Effie's heavy, white breasts, glittering and gleaming in the candlelight, was the answer he had
been seeking for so long, the diamond he had prayed these
last days for his land to return to him.

Never had the desert failed him.

And despite his doubts, it hadn't failed him now. His
fingers slowly traced her neck, then picked up the heavy pink
stone, his face expressionless as finally he held the jewel he
had sought for so long. His mind was whirring. Here was
the reason he had not been able to focus—the desert had sent
the winds, the desert had continually sent him back to her,
back to the stone, back to all he had been seeking.

"This necklace is beautiful..." He was having trouble
keeping his voice even. "Where—" he cleared his throat
"—did you find it?"

"Find it?" His eyes jerked up at the question in her voice. "I didn't find it, it's mine."

"Yours?"

"It's my favorite thing..." Effie smiled, reclaiming the jewel from his grasp and holding it between finger and thumb she gazed at it fondly. "It's probably just glass, not worth a bean, but it means the world to me." She let the diamond drop, and it nestled in its resting place between her creamy bosoms. His eyes were drawn to its magnificence, the candlelight making it glimmer and shine as only a diamond could and he felt awash with fear almost, that she had this in her possession and was completely unaware of its importance. "I wear it all the time."

"You didn't earlier." Zakari pointed out. "I'm sure I would have noticed."

He saw her cheeks pink, a tiny shy smile dancing on her full lips as she answered. "It didn't seem right to, given what we were doing…. It was my mother's, you see—she left it to me...."

There was a frantic conversation going on in his head, warning him, alerting him, to tread carefully, but not by a flicker did he betray his anxiety, his expression nothing more than mildly curious, as he again picked up the jewel between his thumb and finger. Then, holding it in the palm of his hand, he examined it closely and for Zakari there was absolutely no doubt—his search was finally over.

Don't miss
THE DESERT KING'S HOUSEKEEPER BRIDE
by Carol Marinelli!

Copyright © 2009 by Harlequin Books S.A.

Special thanks and acknowledgement are given to Carol Marinelli for her contribution to THE ROYAL HOUSE OF KAREDES series

TWO CROWNS, TWO ISLANDS, ONE LEGACY

A royal family torn apart by pride and its lust for power, reunited by purity and passion

Harlequin Presents is proud to bring you the final installment from The Royal House of Karedes. As the stories unfold, secrets and sins from the past are revealed and desire, love and passion war with royal duty!

Look for:

THE DESERT KING'S HOUSEKEEPER BRIDE
#2891

by Carol Marinelli
February 2010

HARLEQUIN *Presents*

PREGNANT BRIDES

*Inexperienced and expecting,
they're forced to marry!*

Bestselling Harlequin Presents author

Lynne Graham

brings you the second story
in this exciting new trilogy:

RUTHLESS MAGNATE,
CONVENIENT WIFE
#2892
Available February 2010

Also look for

GREEK TYCOON,
INEXPERIENCED MISTRESS
#2900
Available March 2010

www.eHarlequin.com

HP12892

HARLEQUIN *Presents*®

Sold, bought, bargained for or bartered

He'll take his...

Bride on Approval

Whether there's a debt to be paid,
a will to be obeyed or a business
to be saved...she has no choice
but to say, "I do"!

PURE PRINCESS, BARTERED BRIDE

by *Caitlin Crews*

#2894

Available February 2010!

www.eHarlequin.com

HP12894

REQUEST YOUR FREE BOOKS!

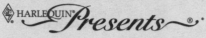

2 FREE NOVELS
PLUS 2
FREE GIFTS!

YES! Please send me 2 FREE Harlequin Presents® novels and my 2 FREE gifts (gifts are worth about $10). After receiving them, if I don't wish to receive any more books, I can return the shipping statement marked "cancel". If I don't cancel, I will receive 6 brand-new novels every month and be billed just $4.05 per book in the U.S. or $4.74 per book in Canada. That's a savings of close to 15% off the cover price! It's quite a bargain! Shipping and handling is just 50¢ per book*. I understand that accepting the 2 free books and gifts places me under no obligation to buy anything. I can always return a shipment and cancel at any time. Even if I never buy another book, the two free books and gifts are mine to keep forever.

106 HDN EYRQ 306 HDN EYR2

Name _____ (PLEASE PRINT)

Address _____ Apt. #

City _____ State/Prov. _____ Zip/Postal Code

Signature (if under 18, a parent or guardian must sign)

Mail to the **Harlequin Reader Service:**
IN U.S.A.: P.O. Box 1867, Buffalo, NY 14240-1867
IN CANADA: P.O. Box 609, Fort Erie, Ontario L2A 5X3

Not valid to current subscribers of Harlequin Presents books.

Are you a current subscriber of Harlequin Presents books and want to receive the larger-print edition? Call 1-800-873-8635 today!

* Terms and prices subject to change without notice. Prices do not include applicable taxes. Sales tax applicable in N.Y. Canadian residents will be charged applicable provincial taxes and GST. Offer not valid in Quebec. This offer is limited to one order per household. All orders subject to approval. Credit or debit balances in a customer's account(s) may be offset by any other outstanding balance owed by or to the customer. Please allow 4 to 6 weeks for delivery. Offer available while quantities last.

Your Privacy: Harlequin Books is committed to protecting your privacy. Our Privacy Policy is available online at www.eHarlequin.com or upon request from the Reader Service. From time to time we make our lists of customers available to reputable third parties who may have a product or service of interest to you. If you would prefer we not share your name and address, please check here. ☐

HP09R

HARLEQUIN *Presents*

EXTRA

**Presents Extra brings you
two new exciting collections!**

LATIN LOVERS

They speak the language of passion!

The Venadicci Marriage Vengeance #89
by MELANIE MILBURNE

The Multi-Millionaire's Virgin Mistress #90
by CATHY WILLIAMS

GREEK HUSBANDS

Saying "I do" is just the beginning!

The Greek Tycoon's Reluctant Bride #91
by KATE HEWITT

Proud Greek, Ruthless Revenge #92
by CHANTELLE SHAW

Available February 2010

www.eHarlequin.com   HPEJAN10

I ♥ HARLEQUIN Presents

BROUGHT TO YOU BY FANS OF
HARLEQUIN PRESENTS.

We are its editors and authors
and biggest fans—and we'd
love to hear from YOU!

Subscribe today to our online blog at
www.iheartpresents.com